Chip Hilton Sports Series
#10

Backboard Fever

Coach Clair Bee
Updated by Randall and Cynthia Bee Farley
Foreword by Dean E. Smith

BROADMAN
&HOLMAN
PUBLISHERS

Nashville, Tennessee

0-8054-1992-6

Published by Broadman & Holman Publishers,
Nashville, Tennessee
Page Design: Anderson Thomas Design, Nashville, Tennessee
Typesetting: PerfecType, Nashville, Tennessee

Subject Heading: BASKETBALL—FICTION / YOUTH
Library of Congress Card Catalog Number: 99-38412

Library of Congress Cataloging-in-Publication Data
Bee, Clair.
     Backboard fever / by Clair Bee ; [edited by Cynthia Bee
Farley, Randall K. Farley].
          p.   cm. — (Chip Hilton sports series ; v. [10])
     Updated ed. of a work published in 1953.
     Summary: When an injury prevents him from joining
the college basketball team, Chip keeps busy serving as an
emergency replacement coach for the high school and partici-
pating in an important basket shooting tournament.
     ISBN 0-8054-1992-6
     [1. Basketball—Fiction.] I. Farley, Cynthia Bee, 1952–   .
II. Farley, Randall K., 1952–   . III. Title. IV. Series: Bee,
Clair. Chip Hilton sports series ; v. 10.

PZ7.B381955 Bag   1999
[Fic]—dc21   99-38412
                                                        CIP
                                                         AC

1 2 3 4 5 03 02 01 00 99

The Chip Hilton Sports Series

For more information on
Chip Hilton-related activities and to correspond
with other Chip fans, check the Internet at
chiphilton.com

TO
the memory of
my beloved nephew
ROBERT "ROCKY" MORGAN

CLAIR BEE
1953

TO

STEPHEN and TRISH SADOKIERSKI:

Great friends,
great parents,
and dedicated international educators.

Love,
RANDY AND CINDY
JAKARTA 1999

Contents

CONTENTS

Foreword

WHEN I was ten or eleven years old, I was forced to read books by my parents. Since I liked athletes, I read and enjoyed several books by John R. Tunis that dealt primarily with baseball but also sportsmanship. Now fast forward to the summer of 1959, when at long last I had the opportunity to meet acclaimed basketball coach Clair Bee.

Frank McGuire was a close friend of Coach Bee, and I had just finished my first year as an assistant to Coach McGuire at North Carolina. Coach Bee was helping Frank with his basketball books, *Offensive Basketball* and *Defensive Basketball*. They had asked me to select two topics for chapters in *Defensive Basketball,* so we spent a great deal of time together that summer at the New York Military Academy.

During this period, not only did I stare at the painting of the fictional folk hero—Chip Hilton—that was on the wall behind Coach Bee's dining room table, but I had the opportunity to read some of the Chip Hilton series. The books were extremely interesting and well written, using sports as a vehicle to build character. No one did that better than Clair Bee (although Tunis came close). By that time, Bee's Chip Hilton books had become a classic series for youngsters. While Coach Bee was well known as one of the great coaches of all time due to his strategy and competitiveness, I believe he thought he could help society and young people most by writing this series. In his eyes, it was his "calling" in the years following his college and professional coaching career.

Coach McGuire and I, along with countless other basketball coaches, learned basketball from Clair Bee. The point zone, which Coach Bob Spear and I developed at the Air Force Academy, had its origins in one of Coach Bee's old books on the 1-3-1 rotating zone defense. We made our point zone at Air Force more of a match-up zone, but this is just one instance where people on the basketball court today still depend on innovations by Clair Bee.

From 1959 until his death, I visited with Coach Bee frequently at the New York Military Academy and at Kutsher's Sports Academy, which he directed. He certainly touched my life as a special friend. Not only does he still rank at the top of his profession as a basketball coach, but he now regains the peak as a writer of sports fiction. I am delighted the Chip Hilton Sports series has been redone to make it more appropriate for athletics today without losing the deeper meaning of defining character. I encourage everyone to give these books as gifts to other young athletes so that Coach Bee's brilliant method of making sports come to life and building character will continue.

DEAN E. SMITH
Head Coach (Retired), Men's Basketball,
University of North Carolina at Chapel Hill

CHAPTER 1

The Air Up There

WILLIAM "CHIP" HILTON would recognize those familiar, sweet sounds anywhere: the rhythmic ping of the dribble and the metallic jangle of the loose basket hoop! But something was out of place. He didn't hear any laughter or shouts of excitement. His curiosity aroused, Chip crossed the street and peered through the mesh of the playground fence. Inside, on the gray concrete court, two middle school boys were shooting an old, lopsided basketball, concentrating desperately on each shot. They were definitely serious.

Chip glanced at his watch and then pushed open the squeaky, rusting gate. "Hi, guys," he said. "OK if I join you?"

Startled, the boy with the ball turned swiftly toward Chip and looked at him carefully. The serious middle schooler noted Chip's strong hands, broad shoulders, and short blond hair. Looking into Chip's keen, gray eyes as he bounced the ball, the boy smiled briefly and then turned and heaved a shot at the basket. "Sure," he called, following the ball and recovering the rebound. "Here! Catch!"

Chip caught the ball and flipped a short jumper cleanly through the hoop. The easy, graceful follow-through of his wrist and fingers captured the youngsters' attention more than the shot's accuracy.

"Man," the taller boy exclaimed in admiration, "that was good!"

"Yeah! Real good," the other echoed.

Chip smiled. "Just luck," he said, following the ball and carefully passing it to the second shooter.

"Uh-uh," the first one said, "that wasn't luck. You've had the fever! What's your name?"

"Chip Hilton. What's yours?"

The boy squared his shoulders and straightened up. "My name's Bobby Bollinger," he said proudly. "Sky Bollinger is my big brother."

Chip nodded gravely, keenly aware of the pride in the voice. "Your brother play basketball?"

"Play basketball?" There was shocked disbelief in the voice. "Play ball?" the little hoopster repeated. "You mean you don't know Sky? Sky's a star! He goes to the university! He's gonna play on the team!"

"What position does he play?"

"Sky can play anywhere! Mostly plays center though. He's seven feet tall!"

"Seven feet!"

"Well, not quite, maybe," Bobby said grudgingly. "But he's awful tall. How tall are you?"

"Six-four."

"You gonna play for the university?"

"I hope so."

"I *thought* you were one of those university dorks!"

Chip laughed. "I'm a freshman at the university," he said, "but I hope I'm not a dork." He turned to the smaller boy who had been listening quietly. "And what's your name?" he asked.

But he wasn't talking. He backed away, his brown eyes suddenly shy, his hands seeking refuge in the pockets of his jeans.

"That's Dickie," Bobby announced gravely. "Dickie MacDonald. I'm teaching him to shoot."

"Is Sky a good shot?"

Bobby's mouth fell open. "Good shot?" he managed. "Sure is! Sky's the best shot in the country. He's the AAU shooting champion!"

Dickie suddenly found his tongue. "That's right!" he said, nodding vigorously. "That's why we've got the fever."

"Fever?"

"Sure! Backboard fever. You know—basketball! My mom says it's a disease. Anyway, just about everybody in University's got it!"

"You don't seem old enough to have this—uh—fever."

"I'm almost twelve years old! I'm in middle school already."

"I'm almost twelve too," Bobby added.

All the time they had been talking, Chip and the two boys had been taking turns with the lopsided ball. Chip's deadly accuracy seemed to hypnotize the boys; they soon gave up their turns to watch this new stranger. Chip was shooting just inside the three-point circle and kept popping shots in one after another.

Bobby, intently absorbed, concentrated on every move Chip made. "Wow," he muttered reluctantly, "you shoot better'n Sky. You think you could teach us to shoot like that?"

"I could try."

"Would you? I'd give my right arm to be able to beat Sky!"

The words leaped out almost violently, punctuated with an emotional intensity that seemed completely out of place on the court.

"Maybe you'd better hang onto your arm," Chip grinned. "You'll need it if you're going to be a good shot. How about Sky? Doesn't he help you?"

Bobby looked down at the surface of the court and bounced the ball several times before answering. "Sky's awful busy," he said evasively.

"That's right!" Dickie said, nodding his head vigorously. "That's right. He's always busy!"

"I guess you wouldn't have time to teach us a little right now, would you?" Bobby ventured timidly. "You see, it means an awful lot to us 'cause we're getting ready for the AAU tournament."

"Tournament?"

"Sure," Dickie explained patiently. "Guys from all over the country come here every year for the championship—and girls too."

"I see. And Sky won the championship last year?"

"Sure did!" Bobby said proudly. "Sky won easy!"

"That's right. He won easy," Dickie agreed. "About all the people around here talk about is Sky. 'Specially Mr. Bollinger. Bobby and I thought maybe if we practiced real hard and got real good we might—"

Chip didn't answer. He took another shot at the basket. Then he turned and nodded. "All right, let's get to it! What shot do you want to begin with?"

"Any one you want, uh, what's your name again?"

"Call me Chip. We'll start right under the basket with the layup, and we'll bank the ball against the backboard. Start here and aim for a spot in that small rectangle on the board. Remember, too, that you take off from your left foot when you shoot with your right hand and, naturally, from your right foot when you shoot with your left hand. We'll skip the left hand for a while. Now try to hit that spot.

"First, though, you've got to hold the ball right, fingers fully spread and very loosely. Another thing: Take a little hop when you shoot, the way you do when you jump rope."

"Jump rope!" Dickie echoed in a shocked voice. "That's girl stuff!"

"Not the way an athlete does it," Bobby said defensively. "Sky used to jump rope."

"That's right," Chip said. "Now let's start with the proper grip on the ball. You've got to learn to spread your fingers and hold the ball without any pressure. Don't let the palm of your hand touch the ball. Here, like this."

Thirty minutes later, Chip was heading toward Assembly Hall where he was meeting some of his friends to watch freshman basketball practice. But he was still grinning about Bobby Bollinger and Dickie MacDonald. Those two sure had a lot on the ball. Smart too! Smart enough to get him to promise to teach them to shoot. Bobby was all fired up about his brother. Chip figured there was more to this shooting tournament than Bobby was telling him.

Backboard fever! Now he'd heard everything! Dickie said everyone in this town had backboard fever and that he'd find out as soon as the season started. Well, it wouldn't be long now.

Chip moved a little faster toward Assembly Hall. This would be the first time since the sixth grade that he had missed any basketball practice, except for his junior year at Valley Falls when he'd been hurt at the end of football season and missed the entire winter season.

BACKBOARD FEVER

I can't believe I didn't pass the physical! I'm sure I'm just sore and need to work out the football kinks.

But Dr. Terring wouldn't clear his physical and had convinced Coach Rockwell it would be better to take it a week or two at a time before making any final decisions about Chip's playing freshman basketball.

Near the end of the freshman football season, Chip had been gang tackled after going out of bounds and was then carried off the field. His legs hurt, but football was a rough game, and he had silently toughed out the rest of the season. But Dr. Terring feared that the constant jarring of his knees in basketball would make the injury worse before it had a chance to fully heal.

Coach Henry "Rock" Rockwell didn't even want Chip on the floor during practice. Yes, he could watch from the bleachers if he wanted, but that was all. The Rock knew Chip Hilton—knew if he got out on the floor with the team, even just to shoot, he'd be running full out and then he'd find himself in some action under the boards. No way!

Well, like Coach said, this forced rest will give me a chance to get ahead with classes, and there are a lot more important things than basketball. But two weeks is an awfully long time! What if the physical therapy doesn't do the job?

Soapy Smith's raucous voice roused Chip out of his deep thoughts. "Hurry up, Chipper. They've started!"

Chip followed his three buddies who had been waiting in front of the gym through the doors and up into the bleachers high above the gleaming hardcourt. On the way, he scanned the players until he located his friend, Speed Morris. The fifth member of the Hilton Athletic Club was there all right, dressed in the freshman workout uniform of white shorts and a reversible red-and-blue basketball jersey.

Years ago Chip's dad had lovingly constructed the Hilton A. C. in their backyard—complete with goalposts, baskets, and pitchers mound. The boys had cemented their friendships playing there through their childhood years and still met at the Hilton A. C. when they were home in Valley Falls.

Chip grinned and waved when he caught Speed's eye. Then he sat down and became so absorbed in the action below that he never moved, never shifted his eyes when Soapy Smith's restless, careless elbow smacked into his ribs. Chip was used to Soapy's exuberant outbursts.

"Is the Rock pourin' it on or is he pourin' it on?" Soapy demanded. "Man! I'm sure glad I'm not out there!"

"Yeah, right!" Red Schwartz murmured sarcastically. "Oh, sure. Just like I am!"

Soapy, always a comic, had a comeback perched on his lips, but a quick glance at his companions warned him they weren't in the mood. They were absorbed in the practice below. Soapy shrugged regretfully and lapsed into silence.

Out on the court, Henry Rockwell was at home. The Rock, a perfectionist and a champion of the value of fundamentals, was a stubborn stickler holding to the premise that intelligent repetition held the secret to perfection. And he was putting his favorite principle to work almost on the first bounce.

With the exception of Speed Morris, the freshmen players on the court knew little about their new coach. But they were in the process of learning—learning that he was all business.

Chip Hilton, Soapy Smith, Red Schwartz, and Biggie Cohen could have told the freshman hoopsters a lot about the Rock. These four, along with Speed Morris, had played for the veteran mentor at Valley Falls High

School and knew his methods, his principles, and his love of basketball as well as they knew themselves. Chip and his friends could have warned them that Henry Rockwell was demanding when it came to mastering athletic skills, that every minute of every practice would be grueling work.

Chip, Red, Biggie, and Soapy knew precisely what was ahead for these freshmen players, but any one of the four would have dashed from his seat in the stands if he could have been out there in a uniform, out there with Speed and the Rock. Red and Soapy had had their chance during tryouts but just hadn't been strong enough to make the squad.

Rockwell's voice was sharp and strong, ringing with expertise and authority as he counted for the hard-running shooting drill: "One, two, and up! One, two, and up! One, two, and up! All right, time!"

With one exception, the perspiring players gratefully came to a halt. The unheeding player dribbled to the basket, leaped high in the air, and jammed the ball through the hoop, hanging on the rim for a moment before letting go and dropping lightly to the floor.

It was an explosive dunk! The movable ring snapped loudly back in place, and the backboard reverberated. The tall freshman player shot his proud eyes toward the rest of the players and to the bleachers to see if the scattering of onlookers had appreciated his performance.

"You, there, son," Rockwell called. "Bill Bollinger!"

The tall, well-proportioned athlete turned lazily and regarded Rockwell with cool eyes. Then his long fingers picked up the ball, and he walked slowly to the group. Only then was it noticeable that he was at least a head taller than the other players.

"Everyone calls me Sky, for obvious reasons."

A brief smile flickered across the lips of the stocky coach as he appraised the towering athlete. "How tall are you, Sky?" Rockwell asked, his voice disarmingly soft. "Six-six?"

Bollinger arched his back proudly. "No, I'm six-nine!" he said shortly. "Six feet, nine inches tall and still growing!"

"Then that explains it," Rockwell said thoughtfully, nodding as he looked up at the defiant player. "Guess the air up there is pretty thin. Perhaps that's the reason you didn't hear me call time."

Bollinger shook his head. "Oh, I heard you."

It wasn't the words as much as the brazen arrogance of Bollinger's attitude that charged the air. The long silence that followed was embarrassing and filled with tension. Bollinger's teammates shifted restlessly, and the smile that had hovered on Rockwell's lips and warmed his eyes compressed into a tight, grim expression.

Chip Hilton leaned back against the steely hardness of Biggie Cohen's shoulder and held his breath. Soapy Smith sucked air in through his open mouth and swallowed hard. "Here it comes," the redhead breathed. "The big dummy's asking for it."

"Dummy is right," Schwartz murmured. "He's a legend in his own mind!"

"Watch this!" Soapy hissed.

Rockwell walked slowly up to Bollinger and took the ball out of the antagonistic player's hands. "Bollinger," he said gently, "I'm going to overlook your insolence because you may not understand how important it is for us to utilize every second of our practice time. We have the use of this gym three hours each afternoon Monday through Friday and two hours on Saturday morning. That means we must conserve every second.

"Once again, I'll repeat the instructions. When I call time, all movement and conversation must stop. Is that clear?"

Bollinger shifted his wavering eyes from the steady insistence of Rockwell's firm look to check out the other players. Here and there he caught a spark of admiration on a teammate's face, but the great majority were far from sympathetic toward his efforts to be different, to show off. So the tall athlete yielded with a brief, "Yes, sir."

It was on the surly side, but Rockwell accepted the surrender and turned to the large whiteboard in front of the bleachers. The players encircled him and listened quietly as Rockwell marked in the next drill, talking as he worked.

Up in the bleachers, Soapy tapped his watch and the Valley Falls foursome reluctantly tiptoed down the bleachers, out of the building, and into the cool November air. Then the long silent voices burst into excited speech.

"Someone oughta cut that big fool down to size!"

"How come the Rock let him get away with it?"

"You see the size of him?"

"Size doesn't mean everything."

"Does off the boards!"

"What's more important, he's the only really big guy on the team."

"Maybe that's why the Rock eased up. Maybe he feels like he's gotta baby the guy along."

"Uh-uh! Not the Rock! He'd can him as fast as the smallest guy on the squad. You know that!"

"Guess you're right. What did you think of him, Chip?"

"I like him."

"Like him? After pullin' a grandstand move like that?"

"I didn't like that, of course. But he's big and he moves well and he's got a nice touch on the boards—and he certainly gets up in the air. I met his younger brother this afternoon, and I agree with him. Sky's got everything!"

"Including an exaggerated opinion of himself," Cohen drawled.

Chip chuckled. "The Rock will take care of that," he said lightly. Then he became more serious. "At least I hope so. It would sure be great if the Rock could have a good year—especially this first one."

"Too bad you can't be out there with the team, Chipper," Cohen said sympathetically, dropping a heavy arm around his friend's shoulders. "How long has Doc Terring told you no practices?"

Chip shrugged. "He said maybe a week or two at the earliest. Depends on the physical therapy treatments. If he doesn't give the OK to Rock, well, I guess I'll have more time to study or work some more for next year's tuition."

"Guess we're all in that same boat," Soapy added dismally.

Cohen snorted. "In your dreams," he said, playfully shoving Soapy. "Chip's in a class by himself when it comes to hoops."

"I didn't mean," Soapy began. "I just—"

"Give it up, Soapy!" Schwartz commanded. "The main thing is Chip's got to get that OK from Terring so he can get out on the court. But I can't believe Rock won't let you shoot around at practice."

"Nope, he said I could watch but couldn't shoot with the team. My practice is the therapy session with the trainer every day. Well, we'll see what happens," Chip shrugged, forcing a smile. "I agree with Soapy. Right now, for whatever the reason, we're all in the same boat."

"Right!" Soapy agreed. "Haven't we always been one for one and all for all?"

"It's one for all and all for one, Mr. Mouth," Schwartz corrected. "Are you still thinking about majoring in English?"

"OK! OK!" Soapy growled, "bug off. Chip knows what I mean."

"Soapy's right, Chipper," Biggie said decisively. "We all want the Rock to get off to a good start, and you've got what it takes. Once you're out there with the team, he can't miss!"

Chip nervously laughed that one off, too, and that's the way things stood when the group reached State and Tenth and the most popular student hangout on the campus, Grayson's. Chip and Soapy hesitated long enough to say hi to Grayson's regulars and then hurried to change into their uniforms: red-and-blue polo shirts and white slacks. As they were dressing, Soapy continued the conversation.

"Chip, do you have any real idea how long you'll be out?"

"No. Doc Terring said we'll take it a week or two at a time. Why?"

"Well, I was just wondering, you know, how you're really feeling about it."

Chip tugged his polo shirt over his head. "There's more to life than basketball, right?" His voice came out muffled. "Let's go, Soapy, the place looked busy when we came in."

Soapy nodded glumly as if agreeing, but he was concerned. *Chip's injury must really be bothering him,* Soapy thought. Maybe it was worse than Chip was saying. Chip was too philosophical, too cheerful. He was trying too hard.

Grayson's had begun as a small family pharmacy, expanded to include a soda shop, and then, with the acquisition of the adjoining two buildings, had evolved into the most popular student gathering place in this college town. The pharmacy was still thriving next door, but the food and fountain areas kept things lively and drew the student crowds. For his newest additions, George Grayson had brought in a popcorn machine, several couches, and a big-screen TV for all the ESPN college sports coverage. As Chip had said, the place was starting to fill up.

The Grayson's regulars were surprised by Soapy's unusual preoccupation that evening. Not that they minded very much. Soapy was extremely liberal with the ice-cream dipper when deep in thought. And tonight, Soapy was concentrating on the toughest problem he had faced during the three months he had been on the campus. Chip seemed on the verge of giving up, and he just couldn't understand it! This wasn't the Chip Hilton he'd known all his life. This injury had Chip worried. Soapy wanted to do something. A solution could result in State having a great freshman basketball team, the Rock a successful season, and—what was most important to Soapy Smith—a chance for his best friend to play the game he loved—basketball!

CHAPTER 2

The "Stage Father"

SKY BOLLINGER was very pleased with himself as he sauntered home through the gathering dusk. He had gotten under Rockwell's skin, and he'd put the old man in his place. He chuckled out loud. That wasn't half of it! He'd just begun! Sky Bollinger wasn't taking any nonsense from any high school coach. Jim Corrigan was his coach. Corrigan understood him. This new guy took himself too seriously. If he'd known Corrigan wasn't going to coach the freshman team, he would've gone to A & M. Well, anyway, he'd be playing for Corrigan next year on the varsity.

Sky's rangy legs carried him up the steps to the porch and into the house in three long jumps. Barging down the hall, he found his mom sitting at the kitchen table, nervously sipping a cup of coffee, and looking out the window.

"Hey, Mom. Where's everybody?"

Trudy Bollinger sighed deeply and looked at Sky with tired eyes. "Your father's out back," she said resignedly. "And Melanie will be late because the cheerleaders are practicing for the alumni game. I suppose Bobby is still over at the playground with his basketball. At least that's where he said he was going. Seems like everything in this house centers on that inflated ball."

"You mean we gotta wait for the brats before we can eat?"

"You know how your fath—" Just then the front door slammed and someone clomped up the steps two at a time. "That's Melanie," she announced gravely.

"Big horse," Sky muttered, peering into the refrigerator and snatching a piece of cold chicken.

"You're going to spoil your dinner," Mrs. Bollinger warned. "Now, if only Bobby would come home, we could have dinner. I wish you'd go get him, Sky."

"Aw, mom, the coach nearly ran us to death. I'm worn out. I think I'll stretch out in the TV room for a while. Gimme a call when dinner's ready, will ya? Man, I'm tired."

Sky's mother quietly rose to her feet. "All right, Sky," she said wearily, "you go ahead."

William Bollinger Sr. was a big, broad-shouldered man in his late forties. "Slats" Bollinger had played high school basketball and was forever telling everyone all about it! Hefting the hammer in his hand and nodding in satisfaction, he contemplated the portable goal with a transparent plexiglass backboard he had just finished assembling. Over the garage door, the old, well-worn wooden hoop drooped in comparison. Wouldn't Sky be surprised! A glass backboard!

He went over to the wooden box he had built for Sky's equipment and took out the new basketball. It bounced sure and true, and the feel of the grained surface filled him with a familiar yearning, taking him back thirty years to the cheers of the crowd:

"Go, Bollinger!"

"Shoot it, Slats!"

"Slats Bollinger scores again!"

Juggling the ball from hand to hand, he resisted the desire to take a shot and placed it carefully back in the box. *No,* he was thinking, *Sky has to take the first shot.* Then, proudly taking one last look at the backboard, he started for the house. Maybe Sky was home. He bet there wasn't another glass board in town this nice except those at the high school and the university.

He was so wrapped up in his anticipation of Sky's surprise that he didn't see Trudy Bollinger until she spoke. "Bill, dinner's going to be ruined! And Bobby's still over at the playground."

"All right, all right! Sky home yet?"

"Yes, he's home. Melanie too."

Bollinger hurried past his wife and into the house, and Mrs. Bollinger started patiently for the playground. Inside, Sky was sprawled on the couch in front of the TV.

"You all right, Sky?" Mr. Bollinger asked anxiously. "You feel OK?"

"Sure, Dad, I feel OK. Except—"

His father's eyes suddenly darkened. "What's wrong, Sky? Something go wrong at practice?"

Sky sat, grinning slyly. "No," he said smugly, "everything went right! The new coach was trying to impress everybody, but I let him know where he stands."

"Good! You'll probably have to carry the whole team on your back. Too bad Corrigan isn't handling the team. I don't understand what they're thinking! They ought to know how important it is to get kids off on the right foot the first year they're playing college ball. By the way, Sky, I've got a surprise for you. Out back. Come on!"

"Aw, Dad, after supper—"

"Nope, right now! This can't wait! Melanie, you upstairs? Get down here on the double! Big event at the Bollinger house!"

Mr. Bollinger led the way out the side door so the view of the garage was obstructed. Trudy Bollinger was just coming up the driveway from the street, followed by Bobby, his basketball under his arm, head down, and shoes scuffling.

"Pick up your feet, young man," Mr. Bollinger reprimanded sharply. "How many times do I have to tell you to be on time for dinner?"

"Sorry, Dad. Mom said supper would be late since Sky and Melanie were practicing, and I thought—"

"Never mind what you—"

"That's right, Bill," Mrs. Bollinger interrupted her husband.

"Well," Mr. Bollinger grumbled, "make it the last time. Now, everybody join hands and close your eyes. I've got a surprise."

Bill Bollinger slowly led his family to the front of the garage, pausing just long enough to excite their curiosity.

"OK! Open your eyes," he commanded and pointed dramatically to the new portable backboard and stand. "What do you think of that?"

"Oh, man!" Sky exploded. "Glass! A glass board!"

"I thought it was a new car," Melanie muttered in dejection.

Mrs. Bollinger and Bobby said nothing. Trudy Bollinger was completely fed up with basketball, and Bobby simply wasn't interested. All he ever heard his father talk about was "Sky this" and "Sky that." Anyway, he was too busy thinking about all the things Chip Hilton had taught him about shooting to care whether Sky's new backboard was made of glass or pure gold.

BACKBOARD FEVER

Later, at the dinner table, Bobby scarcely listened to Sky's description of his clash with the new freshman coach. With each spoonful of mashed potatoes, Bobby was thinking about fingertip control, spots on the backboard, shooting angles, the little hop, and the hand-in-the-basket follow-through that ended every shot. He could almost see himself in Assembly Hall winning the twelve-and-under AAU shooting contest and walking out to the center of the court to receive the championship trophy.

At about the same time, Chip Hilton and Soapy Smith were facing the busiest part of their night's work. Grayson's was jammed, and Soapy loved it! Soapy had access to all the milkshakes, banana splits, and frenzied sundaes he could handle. But even more importantly, Soapy's work at the counter positioned him directly opposite Mitzi Savrill!

Mitzi Savrill, petite, blue-eyed, intelligent, and, according to Soapy Smith, drop-dead beautiful, was George Grayson's efficient cashier and a big hit with the students who stopped in every day.

George Grayson had graduated from State over thirty years ago. He knew how to run a successful business in a college town. That was one of the reasons so many of his employees were students at State—and he liked the idea of helping them as they earned their college degrees. He'd known Mitzi was a winner the first day she walked into the store in search of a job. He'd hired her on the spot.

And he'd been right; she was a real asset to Grayson's. Not only because she was an accurate cashier and knew how to balance the books, but also because she was great with the customers and her coworkers. Mitzi, who was majoring in psychology, had a keen understanding of human nature and kept the customers and employees in high spirits.

But Grayson also liked to hire student athletes whenever he could, and he'd hit the jackpot with Fireball Finley, Chip Hilton, and Soapy Smith. Finley was a great football star. He had captained the freshman team and had proved himself an outstanding fullback. He promised to be a varsity starter next year when he would be a sophomore.

Chip Hilton was undoubtedly the outstanding athletic figure. He had led his championship Jefferson Hall team to startling victories over mighty Oxford and the bitter, time-honored rival, A & M, when the freshman team had been quarantined.

Last, but not the least of the athletes, was Soapy Smith. Soapy didn't look like an athlete. He didn't possess the long, loose-muscled frame of a Chip Hilton or the granitelike stature of a Fireball Finley, but the freckle-faced humorist was as strong! His compact body was enveloped in layers of hard muscle, despite his tendency to put on a few pounds when he indulged himself too often in his ice-cream creations. But Soapy was a cracker-jack football player, excelling as a pass receiver and as a blocker. He was disappointed about not making the freshman basketball team, but he'd already set his goal to make the team as a sophomore.

Soapy was mesmerized by Mitzi's intelligence and good looks. He watched her from afar every possible second. Tonight, Soapy's interest was divided between the disconcerting Mitzi, the rush of orders, and his worries about Chip. Suddenly he straightened up and shouted directly into the face of his startled customer.

"That's it!" he exclaimed, cramming ice cream into the red-haired girl's small Coke and shoving it across the counter.

"What's it?" the girl demanded.

"Mitzi!" Soapy exploded.

"I just ordered a Coke!"

The indignation in the girl's voice snapped Soapy out of his trance, and he quickly looked at her puzzled expression. "A Coke? Sure, coming right up," Soapy agreed, reaching for a glass.

"But what's this?" asked the girl pointing to the glass in front of her.

Soapy looked from the girl to the glass and didn't miss a beat. "Um, that's our newest special of the week, the new campus Coke! You'll love it! This one's on the house. Tell your friends."

Soapy's winning personality and crooked smile had saved him in hundreds of embarrassing situations, and it didn't desert him now. The girl smiled back, asked for a spoon to drink her soda—and that was that!

A little later, when the first lull came, Soapy managed to fight his way past Chip and Fireball and reach the cashier's desk. "Um . . . look, Mitzi," he managed.

"Well," she demanded, pretending a gruffness that was never a barrier to Soapy. "Well," she repeated, "now what?"

"I gotta see you tonight, Mitzi," Soapy stuttered. "Alone!"

"Alone?"

"Um, yes. You see, it's important. It means a lot to Chip and maybe even to the school."

Mitzi's eyes flashed across the store to the fountain. Chip and Fireball were watching every move Soapy made. Fireball put his thumbs to his ears and wiggled his fingers to the astonishment of the student who had just ordered a cappuccino. Mitzi, a little astonished, too, turned back to Soapy.

THE "STAGE FATHER"

"Hmmm. Chip, huh? Well, could you walk home after work with me?"

"Could I? Oh, man! Can a fish swim?"

"And Jane Adams?" Mitzi continued. Soapy's face fell, but only for a second. This was strictly business. Romance could wait!

"Fine," he said. "Fine!"

Soapy's return to his station was a hazardous journey and required quite a bit of footwork behind the busy counter. "Ouch," he wailed, glaring at Fireball and clutching his aching ankle. "What's that for?"

"As if you don't know!" Fireball hissed.

Henry Rockwell opened the door at that moment and probably broke up an argument that the customers wouldn't have understood, but that Mitzi Savrill and Chip Hilton certainly would have enjoyed.

"Hello, everybody," Rockwell said. "How's business?"

"Busier than the Sugar Bowl back home, Coach," Chip quipped. "How's basketball?"

"Not bad."

"We watched the workout this afternoon a little while, Coach," Soapy interrupted. "If you ask me, you're gonna need help. Especially Chip's!"

"Nobody's asking you, Soapy," Chip remonstrated, frowning.

Rockwell smiled understandingly. "Soapy's right, Chip. That might do it. Keep up those treatments with the trainer. We'll let practice take care of itself. But if I know William 'Chip' Hilton, he's taking a few shots somewhere. I just stopped in to say hello and make sure all of you are hitting the books. Got a meeting with the head coach and A.D. Good night."

BACKBOARD FEVER

The administration of intercollegiate athletics at State University was under the direction of D. H. "Dad" Young. Dad was a tradition at State and had built a successful team of coaches and administrators.

After the formal meeting broke up, Jim Corrigan, the men's varsity basketball coach, joined Henry Rockwell, and the two men chatted informally about their respective squads as they made their way across the campus.

"How do they look, Rock?"

"Not bad, Jim. We've got some fine material except for height."

"How about Bollinger?"

Rockwell hesitated. "Well," he said slowly, "the big kid could be great. He's got everything except that he's—"

"Temperamental?" Corrigan suggested with a knowing smile.

"I'm afraid that's it," Rockwell agreed.

"I can appreciate what you're up against, Rock. I guess I know the kid—and his father—as well as anybody. Frankly, they're both a pain in the neck. You probably haven't met the old man yet. But you will! If ever there was such a thing as a stage father, he's it."

"If he's any more of a problem than Sky—"

"He is," Corrigan said shortly. "He'll be running your club any day now."

"The big kid's got a lot on the ball," Rockwell mused.

"That's for sure!" Corrigan nodded. "There were a lot of places after him. Especially after he won the AAU shooting championship."

"How come he chose State?"

"Pressure by his father mostly, I guess. Bill Bollinger loves the limelight, especially when it comes to basketball. He basked in his kid's glory for four years while Sky was playing in high school here in University, and I guess the father couldn't stand the thought of his kid going away for school and leaving him behind. I heard he even wanted to approve interviews with reporters."

"That's why we all make the big bucks," Rockwell laughed.

"Guess I don't have to tell you about the hard work of coaching. I'm sure you could tell me some stories," Corrigan grinned. "Anyway, this is a tough conference. There isn't a team we'll meet that doesn't have a big man—and I mean big! Most of them have two or three!"

Soapy Smith endured, what seemed to him, the longest evening of his life. He watched the clock crawl past eight, nine, ten, and, finally, eleven. Soapy tore past Chip and Fireball on a fast-break dash that took him in and out of the employee changing room in less than thirty seconds. While Chip and Fireball were still looking at each other with astonishment, Soapy reached the cashier's desk, history books and a *Sports Illustrated* under his arm and a smile on his face as wide as Biggie Cohen's back.

As he paraded out the door between Mitzi Savrill and Jane Adams, Soapy found just enough time to flash a triumphant glance at the long faces of Chip Hilton and Fireball Finley.

Later, to the immense relief of Soapy, they left Jane at her dorm and continued toward Mitzi's house. Then Soapy really started in on the subject of Chip Hilton and basketball. Half an hour later, Mitzi managed to get in a few words.

"Is Chip as good as you say he is in basketball?"

"Good? Are you in your right mind? Good? He's Mr. Basketball himself!"

"All right then, enter him in the AAU shooting tournament. That's the biggest winter sports event in this town!"

Soapy's face sobered. "I don't think Chip would go for that. He doesn't like things like that. Besides, I don't see how that's going to help anything."

"You really mean you don't have what it takes to win Chip over—to get him to enter the tournament, isn't that right?"

"Yes . . . um . . . no. 'Course I have what it takes!"

"Well, I thought you wanted my advice."

"I did—I do!"

Mitzi's big violet-blue eyes clouded, and she murmured, "Don't you trust me, Soapy?"

"Trust you?" Soapy sputtered. "Mitzi, I'd trust you with—with my life!"

CHAPTER 3

Like Father, Like Son

BOBBY BOLLINGER was worried. He glanced at the guys with him and turned to scan the street. Maybe Chip wouldn't come. He and Dickie would be embarrassed if their new friend didn't show up. Maybe Chip wouldn't like what had happened when he did come. It wasn't a big deal. He and Dickie had just told some of the high schoolers about someone who could shoot better than Sky, and that had started everything. Lucas Barker, Samuel Burns, and Jackson Grant hadn't believed it and decided to see for themselves.

"Here he comes!" Bobby called excitedly. Then the worried expression returned to his face, and he started for the gate, closely followed by Dickie.

"Hi, Chip!"

Chip greeted the two middle-schoolers and then looked questioningly over their heads to the court where three boys, grouped under the basket, were checking him out.

"They're friends of mine, Chip," Bobby explained quickly. "They wanted to meet you. This is Lucas Barker! He's captain of the high school team. And this is Samuel Burns and Jackson Grant. They play on the team too."

Chip shook hands with the three newcomers, but he was curious. "I can't understand why you guys want to meet me," he said.

"That's easy," Barker drawled. "We just wanted to see the guy who could shoot better than Sky Bollinger!"

"Shoot better than who?"

"You see, Chip," Bobby interrupted hurriedly, "Dickie and I were talking about you at school and some of the guys heard us, and they didn't believe what we said about your shooting and—"

"Don't worry about it, Bobby," Chip smiled. "It isn't very important. I understand." He turned to the others. "I'm far from being a great shot, guys, but I'll be glad to show you anything I know about shooting. I had a pretty good coach. You've probably heard of Henry Rockwell. He coaches the State freshman team."

Bobby hustled after the ball, and Chip snapped it back and forth with the eager little guy until he felt warmed up and loose. Then he grinned and said, "OK, it isn't going to be exactly startling, but I'll try my best. I'll start with free throws if you don't mind."

Chip missed the first one and then ran off fifteen in a row before he missed again. Bobby and Dickie retrieved the ball each time, and when Chip missed on the sixteenth, Bobby explained carefully that the ball was "lopsided and pretty heavy too!"

"How about a jumper?" Barker called, a new respect ringing in his voice.

The jump shot was one of Chip's best shots, but he didn't try to show off by starting from a distance.

He began with short, easy shots, dropping them in neatly with a perfect follow-through of the hands and with the same little hop he had taught Bobby and Dickie. Dropping back a step at a time, he soon was shooting from a distance of more than twenty feet, and he was hitting them almost every time.

"How about some pivot shots?" Samuel asked eagerly, retrieving the ball and passing it to Chip. "That's my shot!"

Chip knew all the moves—the feints, fakes, and shots—and he spent the next twenty minutes explaining the different maneuvers Henry Rockwell had taught him about playing under and around the basket. When he finished, there wasn't any question about what the high school players thought about Chip Hilton. The respect was evident in their voices and in their actions and brought Bobby and Dickie wide grins and shining eyes. That was all the reward Chip wanted.

"Bobby said you could dunk a ball," Jackson suggested.

"That's easy for Chip," Bobby bragged.

"And how!" Dickie boasted. "Chip does it easy! Either hand. Show 'em, Chip!"

Chip dropped back from the basket near the free throw line, took two long strides, leaped up, and flipped the ball down through the ring with his right hand. Then he did the same thing with his left hand.

That was big as far as Barker, Burns, and Grant were concerned. They crowded closely around Chip while he explained that the secret behind dunking was in gripping the ball. "If you can't grip the ball, you can't dunk. Timing plays a big part when you aren't tall. Naturally, it's easy for the big six-six or so guys because they don't have to take much of a jump. Hey! I've got to get going! I'll be late!"

"Would you mind if we came over again day after tomorrow?" Barker asked. "We're only practicing every other day now. We'd sure appreciate it if you'd work with us on shooting."

Chip grinned and nodded his head toward Bobby and Dickie. "It's OK with me," he said, "if it's all right with my agents and partners here. See ya later."

As Chip turned the corner, he looked back. Bobby was in the center of the high school trio solemnly stating they would be welcome but that he and Dickie would prefer to keep the number to a minimum.

Coach Henry Rockwell already had a pretty good feel for what his players could do. And he should have been happy, because he had several excellent candidates for the number-one and number-two spots in his favorite down-the-middle attack principle, and for the all-important under-the-basket position, he had Sky Bollinger.

Bollinger could do everything expected of a big man, and he could do it well. He could leap high above the basket for a tap-in or a rebound. He was one of the best shots Rockwell had ever seen. Furthermore, he was fast, often leading the first wave of the transition all the way down the floor. Too often, if you asked Henry Rockwell. Bollinger belonged under the boards, not bringing the ball up the court.

Yes, the Rock should have been happy. But he wasn't. He hoped Chip would be joining the team soon.

Rockwell had just come from practice and was sitting in his office, somberly moving the plastic players from position to position on his basketball strategy board. He sat there a long, long time, wondering just what he ought to do about the player Jim Corrigan had called the "problem child."

LIKE FATHER, LIKE SON

Bollinger had everything, all right, except the concepts of team play and sportsmanship and an understanding of the value of hard work. Sky loafed in the drills and on defense and was openly defiant and contemptuous. It was difficult to take.

Rockwell showered, dressed, and started for home. As he pushed open the door of Assembly Hall, he bumped right into William Bollinger, Sr.

"Why, hello, Coach. It *is* Rockwell, isn't it?" The big man remained standing in the entrance. "You don't know me, of course, but my son has talked about you so much I feel I know you. I'm Bill Bollinger! Sky's father!" he boasted. "Stopped by to pick him up. Sky says he's been a little tired lately. Guess he's pretty valuable to both of us. Don't tell me I'm too late."

It seemed too much of a coincidence to Rockwell, but he managed a smile. Extending his hand, he permitted Bollinger the satisfaction of displaying his strength. "I'm glad to meet you, Mr. Bollinger."

"Oh, just call me Bill. Slats, if you'd rather. That was the name sportswriters gave me when I played the old hoop game. How'd ya like to have three or four like Sky? Some player, isn't he? Wait till you see him in real action! In the games! Guess he wouldn't tell you, but the kid averaged thirty points a game last year. Yes sir, Sky's the best shot in the country! Won the national shooting championship last year, you know. He's a cinch to repeat this year. Broke all the local scoring records last year too.

"Didn't have anyone to feed him either! With a veteran coach like you handling him, he'll get the ball. It wouldn't surprise me if he averaged forty points a game this year! I'll be over to watch the practices from now on. Now that we know one another. Far's that's concerned, I'll be glad to give you a hand with the coaching."

Right then, right on the spur of the moment, Henry Rockwell made an executive freshman coach decision. "I'm afraid that's not going to be possible, Mr. Bollinger."

"Bill!"

"Bill, then. You see, I expect to conduct closed practices starting tomorrow afternoon."

"Really! Secret practice, eh? You mean even someone like me, a player's father, won't be able to see his own son practice?"

Rockwell nodded decisively. "Yes, I'm afraid that's right! The presence of outsiders at a practice hampers the coach and makes it awkward for the players too."

"But if I helped you coach, I wouldn't be an outsider."

"Sorry, Mr. Bollinger," Rockwell said firmly. "The coaching staff is all set. By the way, the players left long ago. Well, I'd better hurry along. Real basketball weather, isn't it? Sure glad to know you. Good night!"

Bewildered, Mr. Bollinger stared open-mouthed at Henry Rockwell's departing figure. No one had ever squelched him so quickly or so effectively in all his life. "No wonder Sky's been complaining about this man," he muttered. "He's a know-it-all! Who does he think he is? What makes him think he knows all there is to know about basketball? Who does he think taught Sky how to shoot? Bet he never had a son who won the national shooting championship! Nor a player either! If Sky quit that freshman team, this guy wouldn't win a game! I think I'll write Dad Young a letter. No, I'll call Corrigan. He got me and Sky into this mess. Sky had offers from hundreds of colleges, and if it hadn't been for me, he'd be playing at A & M or a dozen better colleges than State. Coaching staff all set! Hah! I'll say it is! Set way back in the dark ages. If I'd known Corrigan wasn't going to coach this team . . ."

LIKE FATHER, LIKE SON

Jim Corrigan got the phone call that evening. He was stuck for nearly an hour listening to Bill "Slats" Bollinger, the old high school hoop star, tell State's varsity basketball coach what the father of the great Sky Bollinger thought of the old has-been the university had saddled itself with and placed in charge of State's basketball future.

After thirty minutes Corrigan decided to sit it out and motioned for his wife to bring him a chair. Then, while Bollinger was talking, Corrigan reviewed the afternoon's practice session in his mind.

Eventually there was a silence, and Corrigan spoke for the first time. "Er—I couldn't hear that, Mr. Bollinger. What did you say?"

That started it all over again, and this time Corrigan paid attention so that he could close it off the next time he got the chance. When the break came, he almost swallowed the mouthpiece.

"Sure, Mr. Bollinger, I'll see him first thing in the morning. You just keep that son of yours out there. Guess I'll have to break off now. The family's just sitting down to dinner. Good night."

Corrigan cradled the receiver and started for the dining room. He sat down just as the phone rang again. This time his wife charged past him, but Corrigan managed to cut her off. "No," he whispered, "you'll spoil everything! Please, dear."

"Hello. . . . Yes? . . . Oh, hello again, Mr. Bollinger! . . . Oh, that's all right. . . . Yes, I guess so. If it won't take long."

Ten minutes later, Corrigan managed to get away and hurried into the dining room to hear the old familiar lecture from his wife and kids. Why couldn't he have been a policeman or a fireman or anything except a captive to a silly game based on throwing a ball full of air through a hoop and spending his nights and weekends consoling fathers who had never grown up and coddling young, spoiled giants who were big enough and strong enough to bounce Jim Corrigan and Henry Rockwell and Dad Young on their knees all at one time? Jim Corrigan knew his coaching profession was sometimes rough on the other people in his house too. Sometimes the best defense was being quiet and eating his dinner.

Soapy Smith got a lecture that night too. From Mitzi Savrill. Right in front of the cashier's desk and right in front of Fireball Finley and Chip Hilton too. Fireball strained desperately to hear what Mitzi was saying. Chip got a kick out of the drama of the triangle and wondered what it had to do with him, judging from the sly glances Mitzi and Soapy kept aiming in his direction.

"Well, when are you going to do it?" Mitzi demanded in a whisper.

"Tonight, Mitzi. I promise."

Mitzi sniffed. "You promised that two days ago!"

"I'll get it tonight! Honest!"

"All right. Remember, the entries have to be in by next Saturday."

Soapy shuffled back behind the counter, perspiring and worrying. He still couldn't see what the entry blank had to do with Chip feeling like his old self or playing freshman basketball. But he knew one thing for sure. Chip wasn't going to sign that entry form unless he applied a lot of pressure. That was what worried Soapy. He didn't know where he was going to get the pressure.

Just then Bobby Bollinger and Dickie MacDonald walked in and swung up on stools in front of Chip.

"Hey, Chip!" they chorused. "How about two gigantic chocolate milkshakes!"

"You got 'em. What are you two doing downtown this time of night?"

"We came down to see you," Bobby explained. "We were wondering if you have to work next Saturday night?"

"No, Bobby. What's up?"

Bobby's hand fished into his back pocket and emerged with a red card. "Here," he said proudly, pressing the ticket into Chip's hand. "Take this! It's for the high school game next Saturday. The varsity against the alumni."

"But won't you or Dickie need it?"

"Nope! Lucas gave us a bunch."

"Sky's gonna play with the alumni," Dickie reported.

"Think you can come?" Bobby asked anxiously, his big brown eyes blinking furiously.

Chip grinned "Sure," he said. "I'll be there."

"All right!" Dickie said. "See, I told you he would!"

The kids downed their shakes, burped loudly, and laughed as they turned and headed out the door—mission accomplished, stomachs full, and hearts happy.

"What was that all about?" Soapy demanded.

"Oh, nothing much. I've been helping those two get ready for some sort of a shooting tournament, that's all. It's a silly idea, but it's all right for them, I guess."

Soapy groaned and glanced woefully toward Mitzi. "Silly idea," he groaned ironically to Chip's astonishment. "You're so right! Lots of silly ideas around here lately."

CHAPTER 4

Gone and Done It!

THE FIRST GAME was only a few weeks away, and Coach Henry Rockwell was still concerned about the freshman team. Bollinger's attitude had not improved. If anything, it was worse. Fridays usually meant a chance to relax from the week's work with a feeling of accomplishment. But not this Friday.

The veteran coach wished he had Chet Stewart, his old high school assistant, to help him work through the situation. He guessed he'd have to let things take their course. But he couldn't help wishing Chip Hilton had received his clearance from Dr. Terring and that Soapy Smith had had a better tryout and that Red Schwartz didn't have to work his way through school. With those three and Speed Morris, it wouldn't matter whether Sky Bollinger and one or two of his followers wanted to work as collegiate athletes or not.

Chip had been working all week with Bobby and Dickie and was pleased by their improvement. The high school players had been over to the playground three times, and he had worked with them all he could.

Rockwell would have been thrilled if he could have seen Chip shooting that afternoon. Chip had never looked better. He was concentrating so intently and Bobby and Dickie were so absorbed that they never noticed the car pulling up just outside the playground gate. They didn't even notice Lucas Barker and a tall man get out of the car. Chip's marksmanship froze the spectators.

"What did I tell you, Mr. Gregory?" Lucas Barker whispered. "Ever see anyone shoot like that?"

The tall man shook his head. "No, Lucas, I never did. Inside and outside too. He's impressive. He should be playing for the university."

"He hopes to," Lucas remarked.

After a few more shots, Chip missed, and Lucas and Mr. Gregory walked to the sideline where Bobby saw them first.

"Uh, hi, Mr. Gregory," he wavered, surprised and with just a trace of alarm in his voice.

Gregory smiled warmly. "Hello, Bobby," he said pleasantly. "Hello, Dickie. You two players mind if I shake hands with your new friend?" He turned to Chip. "My name is Paul Gregory. I'm the principal of the high school. Lucas tells me you're Chip Hilton."

He extended his hand and shook Chip's hand warmly. "You're probably wondering why Lucas and I are barging in on you like this, but the idea is Lucas's. His and Coach Sanborn's. The coach is sick, and he'd like to see you. Have you got time to let us run you up to the hospital?"

Chip was bewildered, and Bobby and Dickie were speechless, probably for the first time in their lives. Chip glanced at his watch to gain time. What was this all about?

"I don't know Coach Sanborn, but I guess so, Mr. Gregory. I have to be at Grayson's before seven."

"Oh, we'll get you there before that. Want to come along, boys?"

The two middle schoolers shook their heads. They didn't want anything to do with a hospital.

"OK, guys. Be sure to say hello to your parents for me."

In the car Lucas Barker explained that Coach Sanborn had been hospitalized for tests and wouldn't be able to be with the team for the alumni game the next night.

"He's determined to win this game just because everyone else thinks we haven't got a chance," Lucas growled.

"The alumni will have Sky Bollinger and Nick Hunter. They both play with the university freshman team," Paul Gregory calmly stated.

Eagerly, Lucas continued. "They've also brought back Tad Steiger, captain of A & M varsity, and Leroy Kelly and Steve Unger who graduated four years ago. They're all big and they're all good. And they all know it!"

"Well, here we are," Mr. Gregory said. "I guess they'll let us in to see him."

"The principal's wife is a doctor here," Lucas whispered. "Everybody likes them."

They followed the head nurse down the hall and entered a private room.

Chad Sanborn looked very sick. His face was gray, and he wheezed when he talked. But his eyes snapped to life when he saw Lucas and the principal. "Glad to meet you, Hilton," he said, his voice rasping. Then he smiled and added, "Excuse me for not getting up."

Chip liked Chad Sanborn. He could understand why Lucas and his teammates raved about him. He was friendly and sincere.

"You rest, Chad," Gregory commanded. "I'll do the talking. Lucas has already given Chip an earful in the car on the way over." He turned to Chip. "I guess you're wondering why we dragged you up here."

"I'm glad I came," Chip said, smiling at the man in the bed. "I've heard some of your players talking about you; they think a lot of you. So, it's nice to be able to meet you."

"Thanks," Sanborn managed, winking gravely. "I wish we could've met in better surroundings."

Principal Gregory came quickly to the point. "Chip, Our JV coach is at a conference. We're in a tight spot. Coach Sanborn and our players want you to take charge of the team tomorrow night against the alumni."

Chip was flabbergasted. He looked from Gregory to Sanborn and then to Barker and back to each again. But words wouldn't come.

Lucas broke the silence. "All the guys want to win this game bad, Chip. And if the coach can't be on the bench with us, we want you! What d'ya say?"

Chip's glance shot to the bed. Chad Sanborn's eyes were friendly and pleased. "That's right, Chip," he whispered. "I want it that way too."

"Me three! That makes it unanimous," Gregory said lightly. "Now it's up to you. We'd be honored if you'd accept."

Chip had mixed emotions—pleased, happy, fearful, and proud all at once. "I'll be glad to help if you really want me," he said, choking a bit on the words. "But I don't see how I can do much. I don't know many of the players or your offense or the defense you use."

"Suppose you just use your own judgment and make decisions on what should be done when the time comes," Gregory interrupted. "That OK with you, Chad? Lucas?" Both nodded and it was decided.

Walking through the hospital corridors, passing patient-filled rooms, Chip's thoughts flew to Valley Falls and his mom. He unconsciously compressed his lips and silently prayed for everything to turn out OK. A few minutes later, Chip stepped out of the principal's car in front of Grayson's, happy to have their confidence and friendship.

After the car pulled away, he stood on the sidewalk a few seconds thinking about this sudden turn of events: from not playing basketball to being a coach with responsibilities for others. He was beginning to believe what Bobby and Dickie had said about backboard fever. Maybe it was contagious. He was beginning to run a temperature himself.

Chip found Soapy in the employee lounge area. "What's up with you?" he joked. "You're fifteen minutes early, Soapy. Are you sick?"

Soapy shook his head mournfully and pointed to the paper. "Friday the thirteenth," he moaned. "Bad luck day for one Soapy Smith." He fumbled with the entry blank in his pocket. "Chip, would—"

"Soapy, listen to this," Chip interrupted, scanning the paper. "The local entries for this silly shooting tournament everybody's buzzing about must be in by tomorrow. Did you ever hear of such craziness?"

Soapy groaned.

"Wait, here's something that *is* worthwhile! Harold 'Bunny' Levitt, the world's free-throw champion, will be here for an exhibition the day of the finals. I've seen him shoot before. He's great! Shoots every free throw underhand. Talk about old time shots."

"Chip—"

"Basketball is a big deal in this town. Look at this headline for the high school game tomorrow night. You'd think they were playing for the state championship instead of a fun game against alumni. They're making as much of a fuss over this game as they are over that shooting thing. Doesn't prove anything."

Soapy moaned. "Chip, I've got something important—"

"What's that? Sure Soa—Whoa, look at the clock! Come on!"

Soapy followed glumly, stuffing the entry form in his pocket. All the way to the counter, Soapy could feel Mitzi's penetrating eyes. This was probably the only time in his life he wanted to avoid looking at her. One quick glance was all it took. Soapy looked away quickly but not quickly enough to escape the big question reflected in Mitzi's face.

Soapy feigned reassurance. Mitzi's face immediately burst into a radiant smile like the sun suddenly breaking through clouds after a dark thunderstorm. Her devastating smile quickened Soapy's pulse, and he forgot everything. Chip chuckled at the spectacle, but Fireball Finley just shook his head in disbelief.

Unlucky Friday or not, Grayson's was packed. Soapy tried all evening to talk to Chip, but an order or someone else always interfered. Then, when Lucas Barker showed up at eleven o'clock with the high school players to walk with Chip to the dorm, Soapy nearly died.

Soapy procrastinated over the equipment, cleaning and scrubbing until the shop lights were dimmed, and then he lingered in the dressing room until George Grayson came in to see what was wrong. Soapy couldn't stall any longer. After the last possible delay, Soapy peeked out the door. Just as he feared, she was still there! Soapy groaned and closed the door. Seconds later he emerged and walked briskly to the cashier's desk. "Here it is," he said forlornly. "Good night."

Saturday was the one day of the week when all the guys who lived in Jeff were around. They took advantage of that day for sleeping late, doing laundry, catching up on E-mails, cleaning their rooms—not very often—or just relaxing. This Saturday morning found Soapy Smith sitting disconsolately on the big porch.

Soapy hadn't been able to sleep. He had gotten up early, tiptoed out of the room he and Chip shared, and slipped softly down the stairs to the front porch and a big easy chair where he could try to figure an "out" for something he had done the night before. It wasn't surprising that Soapy was the first one to get the morning paper—normally a rare treat. He turned to the sports page and scanned the headlines. The high school basketball story caught his eye. Soapy read a few lines and then sat up with a jolt. "What's this all about?"

HIGH SCHOOL OPENS BASKETBALL SEASON
TONIGHT VS. ALUMNI
COACH CHAD SANBORN ILL IN HOSPITAL

University Grid Star to Coach for Ailing Mentor

The basketball season will officially open tonight as the University High cagers host a great array of star graduates in the annual alumni game. Coach Chad Sanborn is hospitalized and will miss the opening contest. William "Chip" Hilton, State's freshman gridiron star, will stand in for Coach Sanborn.

GONE AND DONE IT!

The alumni, overwhelming favorites, present an all-star cast headed by Sky Bollinger, last year's phenomenal scoring wizard and holder of the National AAU basketball marksman championship. Tad Steiger, captain of A & M's varsity, Nick Hunter, a teammate of Bollinger's last season, Leroy Kelly, Steve Unger, Thad Morgan, Rip Henderson, and a host of stars from former years add depth to the alumni squad.

Some of the old old-timers who will be in uniform include William "Slats" Bollinger, Pete Kerns, and Brad Eigen.

There was more, but Soapy had read enough. When had all this happened? How come Chip hadn't said anything about this? That's why those high school guys showed up last night.

Soapy turned back to the paper. Immediately he bolted upright again and stared with shocked eyes at another headline. "Oh no," he pleaded. "Oh no!"

BASKETBALL MARKSMANSHIP ENTRIES CLOSE TODAY

Local Championship Decided Dec. 21
Record List of Entries

Local marksmen competing in this year's National Basketball Marksmanship Championships must have their entries in before six o'clock this evening. All indications point to the largest list of local contenders in the history of the event. The local championships will be held at Assembly Hall on December 21.

Local and sectional champions will be eligible to compete in the national championship finals on Saturday, January 11.

William "Sky" Bollinger, holder of the all-around senior championship, is not required to qualify for the national finals and is not eligible for the local or sectional championship. However, he will certainly be eyeing the competition when the local champion is determined.

University Entries

Coaches Jim Corrigan and Henry Rockwell have entered their varsity and freshman squads intact. Coach Chad Sanborn, local high school mentor, entered his squad some time ago.

A surprise entry is William "Chip" Hilton, freshman QB magician. The football star . . .

"That does it!" Soapy wailed aloud. "Now I've gone and done it!"

Surprisingly, every sports section in every newspaper disappeared that day from Jeff. There was much grumbling from the Jeffs about missing their favorite section, but the newspaper circulation office couldn't explain it. Soapy had had a very busy morning.

CHAPTER 5

Backboard Fever

BASKETBALL! THE fastest growing sport in the world! In every state, in every nation, and on every continent—except Antarctica—the hardcourt game reaches various stages of hysteria during the height of basketball season. Chip Hilton had been in the middle of a mild form of hoop hysteria while starring for Valley Falls and playing on a state championship team, but he had never witnessed anything like the scene he saw as he approached University High School.

The school parking lot was a labyrinth of cars, vans, pickups, and SUVs. The sidewalks were alive with chattering, excited fans, and student groups rimmed the gym entrance selling hot dogs, T-shirts, and school-emblazoned sweatshirts. It took Chip a full twenty minutes to get through the crowd and even close to the ticket window.

"Bet he gets thirty!"

"Not tonight! The kids will run 'em silly!"

"So what! The alumni are too big!"

"What a line! What's the holdup?"

"If I'd thought it was going to be *this* crowded—"

"Me too! They should put this game on TV."

"They ought to do it for all of them!"

"Or build a bigger gym."

"Where do all these people come from anyway?"

Another twenty minutes later, Chip finally reached the turnstile and then made it through only because some older man with an umbrella directly behind him prodded everyone in sight in his wild efforts to get inside in time to "see the last quarter—at least!"

Lucas Barker met Chip just inside the door, but Chip had to use his football knees and his basketball elbows to courteously fight his way through the crowd and across the court to the ramp leading to the locker rooms.

"We can stand here if you want," Lucas said. "I think we'll be able to see. Anyway, we've got lots of time. It'll give you a chance to see the fun. This gym seats seventy-two hundred, but there will be eight or nine thousand in here by the time we start to play."

"How about the fire department?"

"Oh, they're here. Everybody's here!"

"I mean how about the occupancy regulations?"

Lucas shook his head and laughed heartily. "They don't mean anything tonight! No one in this town's got enough guts to close the doors on a basketball game."

The din was deafening. No one was sitting down as far as Chip could see. Everyone in the place was on their feet, shouting, waving, and straining desperately to look over and around those in front.

There didn't seem to be room for another person in the huge, swaying, tightly packed crowd, but people kept coming, shoving, pulling, squirming, and squeezing in somewhere, somehow, until Chip figured a fan in the bleachers couldn't take a deep breath without disturbing someone ten feet away. Everyone watching the preliminary game seemed to go with the flow. From time to time a wave was started, and before long, every fan, young and old, joined in the spectacle, concluding with a wild round of applause and whoops.

Chip was amazed. He had never seen anything like it. "It's backboard fever, all right," he muttered.

Lucas laughed. "Come on, Chip," he said, chuckling, "everyone should be here by now."

The players were all there, some dressed, some just starting, and they gave Chip a grin and a friendly handshake when Lucas introduced them to their new coach.

When they were all dressed, Lucas quieted the team and turned to Chip. "You're the boss now, Coach. It's your show," he said, grinning.

Chip grinned too. "Some show, too," he agreed. "That crowd up there beats anything I've ever seen. Now I understand what University people mean by 'backboard fever.'

"I appreciate all of you asking me to sit on the bench with you. I hope I can do some good. Lucas, you had better make the substitutions. If there are any questions about strategy or decisions, which mean a lot to the game, I'll be glad to help. I guess that's all I have to say."

The players started to rise, but Lucas stopped them. "Wait a minute!" He turned to Chip. "Look, Chip," he said earnestly, "I don't think you understand. This game means more to us than you'll ever know. We've been shoved around and dogged by most of those guys we're going to play against tonight, and we don't like it."

"You got that right!" someone muttered.

"And," Lucas continued, "they'd like to beat us a hundred to nothing if they could. We've got enough pride and belief in ourselves not to like it. We asked you to coach us because we need help. A coach, especially someone like you, someone who doesn't know one of us from the other, can see a lot of things we can't. We've got all the confidence in the world in you, and we want you to take complete charge. Right, everybody?"

The enthusiastic hoots were from the heart, spontaneous and warm, and hit Chip hard. Lucas finished, "I'll give you the starting lineup Coach Sanborn expected to use, and from there you're the general. OK?"

Chip nodded and swallowed hard. Then he was in the center of the circle, joining hands in a silent, tense team grip that expressed a thousand cheers. Chip felt as much a part of this team as any he'd ever known. Then, as if he had finished a little prayer of his own, each player slowly withdrew his hands, and the boys followed Chip and Lucas Barker up the stairs.

Just as they got to the edge of the floor, the band let loose with a terrific blast starting into the introduction to the alma mater, which Chip supposed was the signal for everyone to stand up. But it wasn't necessary. Everyone was already standing.

Right after the last boom of the bass drum, there was a breathless pause, and then the teams dashed onto the floor. The great cheer from the crowd in one long, continuous roar sold Chip on the importance of this game. Lucas didn't forget Chip; he came back and led him to the bench, forcing a couple of overzealous fans to move and make room for the coach.

Mr. Gregory walked out to the center circle and held up his hands for silence. He welcomed everyone to the first game of the season and wished both teams success.

Barker and his teammates were standing and kneeling around Chip when the announcer began to introduce the alumni. The grads got a big hand, and the old old-timers got an ovation, which made them feel years younger.

Then the high school squad was introduced. Chip's ears were burning like fire, but he kept assuring himself that he wouldn't be introduced. There wasn't a point to it anyway. But he was wrong.

"And coaching the varsity, ladies and gentlemen, we want to introduce Mr. William 'Chip' Hilton, substituting for Coach Chad Sanborn."

Chip rose, nodded stiffly, and then sat down quickly. The teams lined up, and the official marched out to the center of the floor. But the ceremonies weren't over. Mr. Gordon Trautwein, mayor of University, managed to get through the crowd and tossed up the ball. Sky Bollinger lazily tapped the ball to the floor. Then, at last, the referee tossed up the ball for the start of the game.

Sky Bollinger, towering far above Samuel Burns, didn't even bother to jump on the opening toss. He just reached up languidly and struck at the ball. Surprisingly, Burns got the tap and flipped the ball to Barker. That didn't bother Bollinger; he smiled condescendingly and followed Burns at a leisurely pace. Sky didn't even lose his cool when Samuel scored, just patted him affably on the back and turned upcourt.

The gesture angered Samuel, but he kept his head and hurried back on the defense, determined to shut down Sky Bollinger. But that was beyond Samuel's power or ability. Sky was too big, too tall, and he had too many shots. The varsity cagers kept pace for a time, but gradually the alumni's superior height, experience, and court sense began to show, and they pulled away. At the end of the quarter the score was 26-12. The varsity dream was over. Every fan in the gym knew that Sky

Bollinger and company could win as they pleased and by as much as they pleased.

Chip kept the starting team in for the entire quarter but substituted Bud Young for Lucas Barker and Dan Johnson for Samuel Burns at the break. While Chip was talking to Barker and Burns, Bollinger sauntered past the bench, snickering, and listened in on their conversation.

"How's the basketball wizard?" he cracked sarcastically. "You don't seem to be doin' so good, Coach. Maybe you ought to use a seven-man team. Don't think it'll help though." He chuckled and walked away.

"I hate that guy. What a bozo!" Barker said bitterly. "What are we going to do, Chip?"

"Just focus on the game," Chip said quietly. "Sit tight and listen. When I put you back in, take a time-out, and I'll tell the guys to slow down the pace and hold the score down."

"We can't win that way," Samuel blurted. "We've got to score!"

"We will," Chip assured the nervous player. "Just do as I say. Never give up! I've got something in mind for the second half."

"OK, Chip," Lucas said grimly, gripping Samuel's arm. "We'll do it!"

"All right, in for Dan and Bud."

Dan Johnson and Bud Young came trotting out, fighting mad. "They're playin' dirty, Chip! Yeah, and you know what? Bollinger said they were gonna beat us by 50 points."

"Maybe," Chip said. "Ignore the trash talk. Now listen, Dan. Go get a room set up where we can use a board and have enough space to move around. We've got to have it for the half."

Sudden hope flashed into Dan's eyes. "Sure, Chip! You got it!"

The alumni starters played the full two quarters without substitutes. Their plan was to run up the score on the varsity in the first half to give the older players an insurmountable lead. At the half the score was 44-20 and the crowd had lost much of its interest. Chip sensed the defeat in his friends' hearts, but in his mind this game wasn't over by a long shot.

On the way to the players' exit, Sky Bollinger pressed close to Chip. "I hope you shoot better than you coach," he said mockingly.

Chip looked at him blankly. More trash talk? What was this guy talking about? He shrugged it off and followed Dan Johnson. The classroom had been cleared of chairs, and Dan beamed when Chip nodded with approval.

Ten minutes later, the same varsity players, but with new attitudes and an energized focus, swept out on the floor as if *they* were the team leading by twenty-four points.

"Well, they've got a lot of enthusiasm anyway," someone observed.

"Haven't done anything with it yet," another fan quipped.

In front of the alumni bench, William Bollinger, Sr., was in his glory. Pete Kerns, Brad Eigen, and he had reported to the scorer's table and were all set to start the second half. Bollinger was waving to his friends in the crowd. It was showtime! Behind him, Chip heard Lucas Barker's father mutter something about both Bollingers being showboats, but he was too busy to pay much attention right then.

Sky stood out of bounds at midcourt, ready to inbound the ball to start the second half. His pass was too soft; Jackson Grant flashed in front of Pete Kerns as though he were standing still and stole the ball right out of his hands. Then Jackson hit Lucas Barker cutting under the basket, and the varsity had a bucket as easy as that.

Sky, Steiger, and Eigen started upcourt after the score, leaving Mr. Bollinger and Pete Kerns to bring up the ball. They didn't get far. Lucas and Stan Moore stuck to Bollinger and Kerns like super glue, applying a half-court press. And it worked! Bollinger passed wildly upcourt, and Bud Young gathered in the ball with a gleeful snort, dribbling straight to the basket for an easy lay-up.

The crowd cheered the two quick baskets, but the Alumni weren't worried. In fact, they didn't even notice the varsity five were working a full-court press until three more interceptions gained three more layups and a free throw. That brought the score to 44-31 and cut the lead from twenty-four points to thirteen. Sky Bollinger called time.

"Here's your new ball game, guys," Chip cried happily. "Come on now, stay right in the press. They'll score a couple. So what! Keep the press on them every second. How do you feel? OK? . . . Good! Don't let up a second. On offense, work the fast break—no threes. Does everybody on the floor remember the signal for a sub? That's right. A clenched fist in the air. Keep them on the run on offense and defense!"

Sky Bollinger was irate. He'd really give it to the varsity wimps. "C'mon, Nick. You, too, Leroy. Let's pour it on! They're high schoolers!"

It wasn't that easy. The grads took the ball out of bounds and started with a rush. But this time they were facing a bunch of high schoolers who were playing a tight man-to-man defense, hustling and rushing every move they made. Kelly fired a high pass to Bollinger under the basket, but the ball never made it. Samuel Burns, playing Sky on the side, stepped in front and intercepted the ball, and away they went, three on two, flying up the court to score on a jumper by Barker near the free throw line. That made the score Alumni 44, High School 33.

Steve Unger grabbed the ball and tried to inbound to Nick, only to find Jackson Grant jumping up and down in front of him, waving his arms and shouting at the top of his lungs. When Steve couldn't find anyone open, he held it too long, and the referee took the ball away from him after what was a good ten seconds rather than the regulation five.

Grant, handed the ball from the official, proved himself an opportunist. He connected with Barker, who was racing away from Tad Steiger, and drove in for another uncontested score. That made it 44-35, and an angry Sky Bollinger called another time-out.

The spectators were excited now, screaming and pointing to the scoreboard. The alumni hadn't scored a point since the half started!

In the last quarter a strange chant began to rumble through the crowd. "Barker, Barker, Barker!" Although the spectators were thrilled by the varsity's strategy and its gallant uphill fight, a new ripple of excitement began to pulse through and through, with the name "Barker" on every beat.

Everyone's eyes focused on the effortless grace of Lucas Barker when he dribbled around Sky Bollinger and drove with lightning speed for the basket. With a quick twist of his slender body, Lucas kissed the ball against the backboard, making it fall through the hoop, scarcely disturbing the cords.

BACKBOARD FEVER

"Thirty-six! T-h-i-r-t-y-s-i-x! THIRTY-SIX!"

The shouts merged into one voice. Barker had scored thirty-six points. He was stealing the show. And the scoreboard lights spelled out the score: Alumni 51, High School Varsity 49.

Chip was surrounded by a howling, screaming, delirious crowd. What a game! He could only watch the flashing lights of the scoreboard and pray for time.

Out on the court, Lucas, Jackson, Samuel, Stan, and Bud were diving and tumbling after loose balls, switching and covering for one another, and playing their hearts out in desperate attempts to get the ball before time ran out.

The hard-pressed alumni, freezing the precious ball, were fighting off the surging, pressing high school players and watching the clock, praying for the end of the game.

Then Lucas Barker took a chance. He tried for an interception and made it! His body dove flat out for the ball, desperation-driven hands clutching the precious sphere. It seemed impossible for the flying figure to regain his balance, to get to his feet without traveling with the ball, but he did it. Somehow, he started for the basket, dribbling furiously in a mad race to beat the big, red digital seconds falling from the clock toward zero. Then, just as Lucas leaped in the air and released a desperation shot, the horn exploded, ending the game—and Sky Bollinger hit him!

CHAPTER 6

Never Give Up

PANDEMONIUM! A deafening roar numbed his senses, and Chip was out on the floor, carried along by a crowd headed for the tangle of bodies threshing on the floor behind the basket. Somehow, someway, someone pulled the contestants apart, and then the crowd saw the red smear running down Lucas's face from the cut above his right eye.

Pushing and elbowing a path through the curious crowd, Chip led him to the bench. The trainer was already there, his kit open on the bench, and Chip and Lucas's teammates waved the crowd away. As soon as he saw the cut was superficial and Lucas was all right, Chip checked on the game.

The scoreboard still read Alumni 51, High School 49, and Chip tried to locate the officials. That ball had gone through the basket! Fighting his way through the milling crowd to the table, he found the two officials checking with the timekeeper.

"Ball was in the air!"

"You sure?"

"Of course I'm sure! The ball had left his hands when the horn sounded!"

"Is that right, Mr. Schultz?"

"Yes, sir!"

"Then the goal counts!"

"That's right!"

"You want me to make it a tie score?"

"Of course! The basket counts! And—"

"What about the foul?" someone yelled.

"Two shots!" another barked. "That was an intentional foul if I ever saw one."

"Up to the official! He's callin' the game!"

The officials weren't going to be drawn into that argument. The referee held up one finger. "Basket counts and there's *one* free throw coming," he said decisively, heading for the foul line. "Foul's on Bollinger."

Just then the scoreboard ticked twice, and everyone looked to see the lights flicker, and there, side by side, were two big 51s: Alumni 51, High School 51.

A great cheer went up then, and that was the signal for the high school jazz band to come to life with a victory march. The music swelled above the crowd and brought some semblance of order to the hysterical gathering. At least for one little second!

Chip turned back to the bench and then he saw the spectacle. Slats Bollinger, looking ridiculous in his short basketball pants and skimpy jersey, was backing away from a short, fat, balding man swinging away for all he was worth, even though he was only fanning the breeze. It would have been funny in any other circumstances. But not here and not now!

Principal Paul Gregory quickly moved between the two parents, pushing them apart. The crowd was more amused than anything, and everyone laughed and joked as the men were forced apart.

"Now, now," Gregory said to the little man who was still fuming and full of fight. "Now, now, Mr. Barker, calm yourself. Calm yourself. Remember your blood pressure."

"I shoulda popped the jerk," Mr. Bollinger raged, now that he was firmly held by two teammates. That remark fired up Mr. Barker with new zeal, and he wrestled himself free and hurled his body toward Bollinger. This time, two spectators grabbed Barker and led him back to his seat behind the high school bench. Lucas, holding an ice pack above his right eye, quieted his father, since Mr. Barker could see then that his son was all right.

Over on the other side of the scorer's table, Sky was sympathizing with his father and glaring angrily at the high school bench. "The little squirt hit me," he griped angrily. "What a joke! Trying to get tough with me! Next time, I'll really let him have it."

Before things could get any further out of hand, the referee called Barker to the free throw circle. Strange how a decisive game situation can change a boisterous, chanting crowd into a tense, silent assembly. Instead of shouts there were whispers, and when Barker walked out to take the ball, a sympathetic cheer rang out spontaneously from practically everyone in the gym.

As Barker stepped up to the line, the crowd noise died as if a great music conductor had lifted his hand. It was a dramatic moment, vital to the alumni and their supporters and important to the high school varsity because it meant a bitterly won victory, a victory snatched from the very jaws of defeat.

Just as Chip had taught him on the playground, Barker stepped to the line, toed it carefully, bounced the ball three times, hesitated with a deep breath, and flipped the ball toward the basket. The path of the ball was true. It followed a perfect arc and passed through the ring with just a whisper, scarcely touching the cords. The thundering roar from the crowd celebrated the success of a "never give up" bunch of kids. They had fought back under a terrific handicap to pull a game out of the fire that no one thought they had a chance to win. Except for the tall, good-looking young coach they hoisted on their shoulders and carried to the locker room.

Chip managed to scramble down at the door to the locker room, feeling foolish and silly, but Lucas, Jackson, Samuel, Stan, Bud, Dan, and the rest of them weren't going to let this victorious coach get away. Playfully, they pulled him into the locker room.

"Don't you go away," Lucas Barker commanded. "We're not finished yet!"

"Don't move or we might miss!" Samuel joked.

Chip didn't move. He just sat there and waited while jerseys, socks, and basketball pants flew from all directions. Just then, Bobby Bollinger and Dickie MacDonald came flying through the door and sat down beside Chip in time to get pelted with the last wave of clothing.

"Chip," Bobby gushed happily, "that was some game!"

Dickie nodded emphatically. "Some game is right! We knew you'd win though. We weren't worried."

"Not even at the half!" Bobby added.

"You see our names in the paper?" Dickie asked.

Chip shook his head. "No, I didn't, Dickie. Why are you in the paper? When?"

"This morning," Bobby said. "The shooting tournament! Yours was there too!"

"Mine? Oh, hi, Mr. Gregory."

"Chip, that was a great game. Congratulations. I don't know how you and the players did it. How about going up to see Coach Sanborn with me? What do you say, Lucas? OK? Good! You're just the guys to cheer him up! Besides, someone ought to tell him about the game. Can you join us, Chip?"

"Sure."

"All right, everyone going be out front in fifteen minutes. It's late, but I think we can make a short visit."

Chip said good night to Bobby and Dickie and piled into Mr. Gregory's van with Lucas, Jackson, Samuel, Stan, and Bud. On the way they replayed the game from the tip-off to the last game-winning shot. But the happy players weren't leaving Chip out. They gave him all the credit.

"Chip did it," Lucas said happily. "I gave up cold!"

"Didn't look like it to me," Mr. Gregory said sincerely. "A player who gets thirty-nine points wasn't giving up in my book."

"That didn't mean anything," Lucas said with embarrassment. "Aw, everybody was feeding me. My dad could have made those shots."

"Not that last one," Chip said. "You saved the best shot until the last. I still don't know how you got it away."

Lucas laughed. "That was luck," he said. "I knew there were only a few seconds left, so I just closed my eyes and let it fly."

Mr. Gregory cleared his throat. "Lucas, what happened when Sky fouled you on that shot? When you two tumbled out of bounds and into the crowd? I couldn't see a thing."

Awkward silence. Gregory was sorry the instant he asked the question. Chip was thinking Sky's foul could have been an accident, the result of playing hard, or it could have been deliberate.

"Why, he pun—" Lucas stopped, mentally kicking himself. He had nearly made a mistake, he was thinking. The game was over.

"He fell on top of me and . . . well, he's kinda big and my head hit something hard, and for a second I thought I was in a fight. Sky must have thought I was crazy."

"I saw you talking to him right after you shot the free throw," Mr. Gregory said. "I wondered what you were saying."

Lucas grinned to himself in the darkness of the van. "I just said it was too bad and that he'd played a great game, that's all." Lucas didn't exactly tell everything about that brief exchange with Sky Bollinger. Sky had ignored Lucas's outstretched hand. He had turned away and said, "What do you want from me, loser? You won, didn't you? With fouls and dirty basketball."

Sky Bollinger was whining the same song seated in the back seat with Bobby and Melanie. Sky was griping bitterly and, at the same time, condemning the high school players and the officials.

"They fouled us all over the place! Grabbing, pushing, tripping. If the officials had had any guts at all, there wouldn't have been any game! They'd all been out of the game on fouls."

"That wasn't basketball; it was a free-for-all," his father concluded. "Probably that jerk's fault who took Sanborn's place tonight. Self-important jerk!"

Bobby coughed and squared his shoulders.

"I'll say he is," Sky agreed. "Got a few lines of ink in the paper during football and his head swelled up as big as a basketball. I hope I get to shoot against him in the tournament."

"Is he in the tournament?" Mr. Bollinger asked incredulously. "He can't be much of a shot. He isn't even out for the team."

Bobby had been squirming and biting his lower lip ever since Chip's name had been mentioned. His fists were doubled up tightly, and he edged as far away from Sky as possible. But he kept quiet. He knew his father's moods, and he knew this was not the time to say anything about his own plans. Not the time to get in the middle of this no-win situation. But he couldn't sit there and let them talk that way about Chip. He couldn't hold back any longer.

"He hasn't been cleared by some doctor!"

The car swerved dangerously.

"What's that?"

Bobby felt Sky's body tense, and in the flashes of the passing headlights he could see Melanie leaning forward and peering at him with her mouth wide open. He braced his elbow against the armrest and said it again, louder.

"He hasn't been OK'd to play!"

"Who isn't OK to play?"

"Chip Hilton!"

The car swerved again.

"How would you know?"

"I meet him at the playground."

"Playground?"

"Playground?" Sky echoed.

Bobby took a deep breath. He was in for it now. "Yes, sir."

Mr. Bollinger pulled the car to the curb. This wasn't going to be good news for Bobby. "Now," he began in that voice, "suppose you just tell us all about this Chip Hilton and the playground."

It took a little telling, followed by a lot of questioning, but Mr. Bollinger eventually learned all about Chip Hilton helping his youngest son and Dickie MacDonald with their basketball skills. That Chip had coached most of the high school players with their shooting, and that he was the best shot Bobby had ever seen—with no exceptions!

But Mr. Bollinger didn't learn that there would be another Bollinger entrant in the AAU competition. Bobby decided he might as well hold that out for his mom, and mom alone. Just as Bobby expected, Sky and his father went ballistic.

Chad Sanborn was propped up in bed, reading, when Paul Gregory and most of the varsity strode victoriously into the room. Although Mrs. Sanborn had phoned the score to her husband, she'd been so vague on the details of the final moments that Chad's curiosity had gotten the better of him. He fired questions at them right and left for nearly an hour. It was nearly midnight when they left.

"Thanks again, Chip," Chad said warmly. "I feel so good right now I could play an overtime game without a deep breath. I'll probably get thrown out of here first thing Monday morning. Anyway, in case I don't get to see you, I want you to know I'll be pulling for you next Saturday."

In the van Chip tried to figure out why Coach Sanborn would be pulling for him next Saturday. The jubilant conversation turned to another basketball topic, and he soon forgot about it. Then, as each player was dropped off at his house, Chip's thoughts turned to home.

CHAPTER 7

Blond Bomber

SOAPY CUT the plastic string holding the stack of Sunday newspapers on the front porch. He frantically flipped through the top paper until he came to the sports section. The story he was looking for jumped off the pages. Stretching completely across the page was the headline: COMPLETE LISTING OF AAU ENTRIES. Soapy scanned down the page until he came to the names beginning with H. There it was, second from the top. Soapy groaned and resolutely began clipping those thirteen letters, WILLIAM HILTON, out of all sixty-three papers.

Pete Randolph, Jeff's resident adviser, always enjoyed the Sunday paper first thing in the morning. Opening the door to see if the papers had been delivered, he grunted angrily.

"Soapy, what's going on? What are you doing with all those papers?"

Soapy gulped, ceremoniously grabbed an uncut paper from the bottom of the pile, and handed it to the questioning RA. He gulped again and said he was only cutting a tiny sliver out of each one and it wouldn't be missed because he could hardly see where it had come out. Pete Randolph just shook his head, rolled his eyes and muttered, "Freshmen. How did we let this one in?"

Chip was surprised by Soapy's devotion that day. The freckled redhead shadowed him wherever he went. He never left his side for a second, kept him busy, suggesting this and that and anything that would take Chip's thoughts away from the sports pages. But Chip wanted to read what the papers had to say about the high school team's victory, and Soapy was forced to endure the agony, waiting to see if Chip read the list. Soapy should have been pleased Chip never read Birdie Byrd's campus gossip column, but, unfortunately, Soapy missed it too.

Whenever the guys got together, Soapy usually monopolized the conversation, but today, when Biggie, Speed, and Red joined them just before lunch, he did *all* the talking.

"How's practice, Speed? Coach needs Chip out there, doesn't he? I thought so. Suppose you guys are gonna elect the Skyhawk your captain, huh!

"Get a raise this week, Red? You shoulda taken that job at Grayson's. You qualify on half the title anyway— soda *jerk!* Get it? Ha-ha!

"Don't see how you can work those hours at UPS and go to school the next day, Biggie. Even though it is only twice a week. Man, you're fallin' away to a mere 250 pounds. I'm starting to worry about you! Hah!

"You guys meet the victorious coach here? Ahem. I'm thinking about getting him a shoe contract. Ahem!

"Oh! Did I tell you that before you stands a gentleman and . . . and a scholar? Perhaps you are not aware that this talented individual was the *only* recipient of an A+ on the biology midterm. Ahem."

Schwartz couldn't stand it anymore. "Stop!" he shouted. "You're driving us nuts! You told us—and probably everyone else in town. Motor mouth, if you keep this up, we're going to get you a muzzle!

"What's with you this morning, and why choose us for your audience?" Red smacked his forehead then held up his hands. "Stop! Don't answer that! My mistake!"

"I think it's too much caffeine," Biggie cried. "Now you keep quiet, Soapy, just for two minutes, and you can have my dessert."

"Well! I've never been so insulted." Soapy complained.

In unison, the table shouted, "Yes, you have! Give it a rest!"

Speed tapped the paper. "Lucas Barker must have been in the zone last night, Chip. He that good?"

"He's good," Chip smiled.

"It must have broken the great Bollinger's heart when Barker got all those points," Speed mused. "Wonder what his alibi will be?"

"He can score," Chip said softly.

Speed chuckled. "That reminds me. Rock entered us in this AAU shooting deal that Bollinger won last year."

Soapy choked on his next bite, but everyone ignored him.

"Seems senseless to me," Chip declared. "The Rock's probably chuckling too. He's always talking about practice players, guys who never miss in practice but can't buy a bucket in a game."

"Speakin' of practice," Soapy, clearing his throat, interrupted hastily, "since you got time, when you gonna call Jeff's practice? The dorm schedule starts January tenth."

"That's a long way off," Schwartz assured. "No dessert for him, Biggie."

"Forget the dessert, and it isn't a long way off. Christmas will be here before you know it, and next term starts on January sixth. Jeff's first game is January eighth. And that, my fine-feathered freshman friends, leaves us hardly any time for practice—even if we practiced every day, which we can't and don't!"

"He's right," Schwartz declared. "Where's the semester gone?"

"Slipped up on me," Chip said. "We'll have a chalk talk this afternoon at four o'clock."

There were some pretty good basketball players in Jeff's lounge that afternoon. Red Schwartz and Soapy Smith had played with Chip at Valley Falls, and the Big Reds had been good enough to win the state championship in their junior year. The team had led Section II in their senior year but had lost out in the final game because of a courageous trek through a snowstorm, carrying several armloads of stranded kids. Their championship hopes had been blasted that night after a bitter battle because the Delford coach, Jinx Jenkins, insisted on playing the game even though—and probably because—the Valley Falls players could scarcely move. Delford won in a strange set of game-ending events and went to the championship tournament, but Jinx Jenkins lost his job because of his unacceptable behavior.

Chip didn't know too much about the ability of any of the other players sitting in front of the board, but he did know Jeff wasn't going to use a pivot attack. There wasn't anybody tall enough in the whole dorm except Joel Ohlsen and Biggie Cohen, and neither of the giants played basketball.

"I hope you guys don't mind if we use Coach Rockwell's style," Chip began. "It works, and that's really the only one I'm comfortable with.

"We'll start with shooting. This diagram will outline the shooting areas and the types of shots you should use.

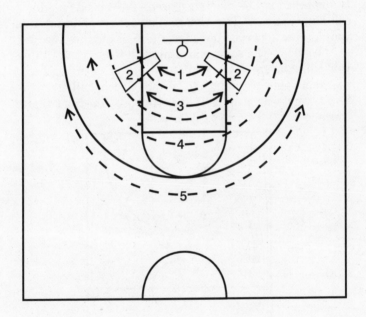

BACKBOARD FEVER

"I'm not much of an artist, but I guess you can follow the diagrams without too much trouble. Unless you're going to dunk it, area 1 is the bank-shot area. All under-the-basket shots should be against the backboard. Remember, put the ball in the box—the rectangle on the backboard.

"The areas marked by rectangles on each side of the basket are also bank-shot areas, just farther out. Each one is numbered 2. The horseshoe area—3—is used for what I call baby-jumpers. The semicircular area, numbered 4, is your jumper, and everyone's favorite, 5, is the three-pointer.

"We'll use the same warm-up drill Rock used. I think you'll like it, since you can use every pass there is and everyone gets a chance to shoot. Coach called it the 'three-lane' warm-up drill. Just in case you can't figure this one out, I'll try to explain it.

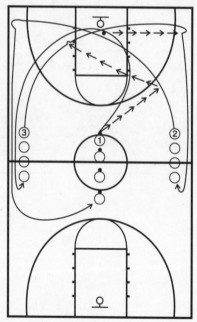

BLOND BOMBER

"Player 1 passes to 2 who passes to 3. Player 3 shoots a baby-jumper or a layup and continues to the right-hand corner. Player 2, after passing to 3, goes to the left corner. The original passer, 1, follows his pass and takes the rebound. Then he passes to one of the cutters, player 3 in this case, and goes up the side. Then the next wave starts.

"I've been thinking about a defense, and I think we'd win a lot of games if we mastered the full-court press. It's a tough one to master, but it's sure effective. I'll put it up here on the board and then try to explain it. Maybe some of you read about the high school and alumni game last night. The alumni were pretty tough, and I don't think the high school guys could have won if they hadn't changed to the full-court press at the half—"

"Seems to me I read that the coach of the high school team had a little something to do with that strategy," Eddie Anderson said pointedly.

Chip smiled but ignored the interruption. "Anyway, it takes quite a bit of practice to master, but it sure gives a small team an advantage. Since we don't have any real big men, well, I think it's the best we can use. It's based on man-to-man principles with a lot of switching.

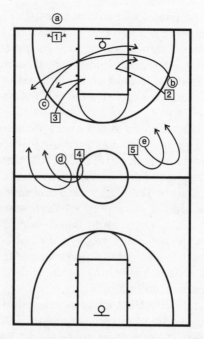

"An opponent, A, has the ball out of bounds following our score. Player 1 plays him tight, waving his arms and trying to make him throw a bad inbounds pass or a throw-in violation. The rest of the players team up man for man, 3 playing C, 2 guarding B, 4 opposing D, and 5 sticking to E. All the time you guard your opponent, you keep an eye out for the pass, and if you think you can intercept it, you make a try for it.

"Now, one more thing. Whenever the opponents cross, as B and C are doing here on the board, you switch opponents and be sure to tell your teammate. In this case, 2 follows B until C crosses, and then 2 changes to C and 3 takes B. Got it?"

BLOND BOMBER

"What do you do when the other team gets the ball inbounds or across the ten-second line?" Eddie asked.

"Continue to play the same way, man to man, but switch every time there's a cross. Play them tight."

"In high school, our coach used to use the press when we were behind in the last quarter," someone said.

"Lots of teams do that," Chip agreed, "but it takes a lot of conditioning and guts to keep it up a whole game. That's why I think it will be successful for us in the dorm league. Most of the teams won't be in shape and will rely too much on shooting—probably threes. We'll be ready."

"You can say that again," Joel Ohlsen remarked. "The Dawn Patrol rides again."

Chip laughed. "Now, we ought to have two out-of-bounds scoring plays under our basket and two sideline plays to get the ball in. These should be OK.

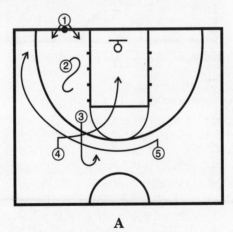

A

"In A, player 1 takes the ball out of bounds. Player 2, usually the center, faces him, standing about six feet away. Player 3 holds his position until 4 and 5 have scissored, then backs up for safety. The pass should be made to the players in the order of 4, 2, 5, and as a safety valve to player 3.

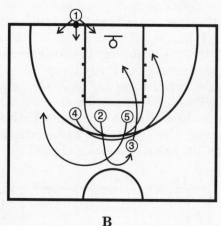

B

"In B, player 2 delays until all three of his teammates, 5, 4, and 3, have cut toward the base line. The pass should be made to 3, 4, 5, and 2 in the order I've named.

"Play C is a good one. The big man should play in position 2, and the pass should be made to him. Player 4 turns and sets a screen for player 5. If the pass is not made to player 2, player 5 cuts to the backcourt and takes the ball. If players 2 and 5 are both covered, the pass is made to 3, who starts for the basket and comes to meet the ball. Any questions?

BLOND BOMBER

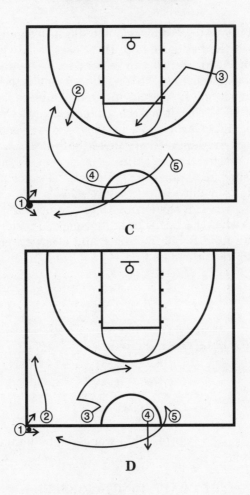

C

D

"Play D is used by A & M. I think that's where the Rock picked it up. The way it's set up here, player 5 cuts first, then 4 drops across midcourt as the safety valve. Player 3 steps toward 2, then reverses to the free throw line as 2 moves toward his end line. It's also a quick scoring play if the ball goes to 2. He passes to 3, who then cuts to the hoop. Signals can be used to designate different players for cutting. We'll work those out later.

"That's it, guys. Joel's trying to find a place for practice, and he'll post it on the bulletin board. Our first game's against Garfield, Wednesday, January eighth, at four o'clock in Alumni Gym. Guess that's it."

Chip started up the stairs to do some studying, but Biggie yelled up to him from the porch. "Here's a note for you, Chip. Some little kid left it for you."

Soapy was still shadowing Chip and peered over his shoulder when he opened the envelope. Inside was a short note from Bobby Bollinger and a newspaper clipping. Chip read the note first.

Dear Chip,

I'm not allowed to practice anymore at the playground. I'll try to see you tomorrow.

BOBBY

P.S.   Here's an article from today's paper. Maybe you didn't see it.

What's Bobby up to? Chip wondered as he unfolded the clipping.

THE CHATTERING SCRIBBLER
by Birdie Byrd

It's b-a-a-a-ck! Backboard Fever is back! This year's seasonal epidemic broke out at the high school last night when Sad Chad's Kids of Destiny came

BLOND BOMBER

from far behind to close down the highly favored alumni stars. The surprise of the game was the unveiling of a scoring phenom, Captain Lucas Barker, who tallied thirty-nine points to set a new scoring record.

By the way, William "Chip" Hilton, State's freshman QB sensation, better known to gridiron fans as Mr. Toe, subbed last night for hospitalized Chad Sanborn as coach of the Kids. High school fans credit the popular State athlete with the victory.

The big "shooting" tournament is here again . . . local eliminations Saturday, December 21 . . . Defending champ Sky Bollinger is in for a *sur-r-r-prise*. Confidentially, this column is choosing a dark horse . . . backing him against the field. Chip Hilton, the Blond Bomber, submitted his entry blank late last night. He played a lot of basketball in high school . . . enough to lead the entire country in scoring.

More than three hundred entries . . .

"Blond Bomber," Chip muttered angrily, staring in disbelief at the clipping. "Where did this come from? Submitted his entry blank last night! To whom? What entry blank? Someone's got some explaining to do."

Later, after their lights were out, Chip reflected aloud. "Must be a mistake. It's got to be some kind of mistake!"

Soapy's muffled voice from under his covers could scarcely be heard. "I'll say it was a mistake."

CHAPTER 8

Chip Sees the Light

WILLIAM "SLATS" BOLLINGER, the old pro, glared across the breakfast table the next morning and repeated the question. "Young man, who gave you permission to enter the tournament? Someone must have. Your name was in the paper."

Bobby wasn't talking. The way Bobby looked at it, he had already said too much. Looking down at his plate, hands folded in his lap, he was surrounded, trapped, caught in the middle between his father and Sky.

"Talk about disrespect," Sky said, his voice filled with contempt. "Imagine the little wimp thinking he can compete. It's a disgrace! He'll make us look stupid. Ask him again who signed the entry blank, Dad."

Trudy Bollinger was usually a quiet woman. Some time ago, she'd surrendered her voice in family problems to her husband. Now she startled the entire family. "I signed the blank, Bill," she said softly. "Lots of boys and girls Bobby's age are entered."

"It isn't just that he's entered," Mr. Bollinger fumed. "It's the disgrace. He doesn't have Sky's athletic ability. Besides, he won't practice."

Bobby opened his mouth to speak and thought better of it. *What was the use? Won't practice? I was until I was told I couldn't go to the playground anymore! And if I'd even touched Sky's crummy ball or used his precious backboard, I would've been sent to Siberia.*

He concentrated on his father's words. "Sky has practiced and practiced every day for years. Did you ever practice something every afternoon until your tongue hung out and you could hardly lift your feet and then you had to walk home with every step an ache and a pain? Did you? Even in the rain, cold, or hot summer?"

Mrs. Bollinger smiled. "No, Bill. Of course not. But if it's that hard on Sky, maybe he ought to give up basketball."

"Drop out of basketball! Are you crazy?"

"Sometimes I think this whole family is crazy. Basketball crazy."

Soapy was going crazy. He tried to work out a solution to his predicament, but the only one he could come up with was a complete confession. But he was afraid. Soapy valued Chip's friendship almost as much as his parents' love. Chip was upset about the entry form and might be badly hurt if he knew Soapy was so concerned about getting a girl to pay attention to him that he would pull such a dumb stunt.

When Chip left for his eight o'clock economics class, Soapy tagged along, trying to build up enough courage to tell Chip the whole story. But he just couldn't get the words out, and the opportunity passed.

Soapy was really desperate now. Chip said he was

going to the *Herald* right after lunch to find out why the paper had included his name in such a frivolous, inane event.

"I've got to find Mitzi," Soapy breathed. "She got me into this mess, and she'll have to get me out!"

Finding Mitzi wasn't easy. She led a busy, popular life. Mitzi was one of the top academic students in her class and also active in extracurricular campus activities and groups. Off campus, Mitzi wrote a column for the *Herald,* worked as bookkeeper and head cashier at Grayson's, and wrote short stories for young readers.

Soapy nearly ran his legs off, but he finally found her in the cafeteria in the student union. She was enjoying a salad and deep in conversation with five junior classmates. That meant nothing to Soapy. He barged right in.

"Mitzi! I gotta see you! Right away!"

Soapy was so glad to find Mitzi that he never gave the usual courtesies a thought. He didn't even see the junior males stand up around him.

"Excuse us, but aren't you a freshman? You just have to be. Can't you see this is a study group, and we're having an important discussion? Not to mention our lunches."

Soapy quickly glanced in their direction and then backed away. "I'm sorry, guys—er—gentlemen, but it's an emergency. It's about Ch—It's a personal matter of life and death nearly. And Mit—I mean, Ms. Savrill—is the only person on campus who can take care of the situation and help me."

"Go on!"

"Um—that's all."

"Sounds good to me, Andy."

"We'll see."

"What's your name, freshman? What's your dorm?"

"Soapy Smith. Jeff."

"How can we be sure? Let's see your student ID."

There were beads of perspiration on Soapy's forehead as he searched his pockets and eventually produced the precious card. One of the upperclassmen examined it carefully, enjoying Soapy's discomfort.

"He's who he says he is."

"All right, freshman. My name is Andy Thornhill. I'm president of the junior class. The gentleman on my right is Don Santos. The gentleman on my left is Kirk Barkley. I'm quite sure you realize that you have violated a number of State University's points of etiquette in the past few minutes. Are you prepared to pay for your mistakes?"

Soapy gulped. "Yes, sir."

"Excellent! We were hoping you'd say that. We'll pick you up at Jeff tonight at seven o'clock sharp!"

"All right. I mean, no! I have to work. I have a job. Ask Mit—ask Ms. Savrill."

"Is that right, Ms. Savrill?"

Soapy was surprised. "Hey, I've waited on you a lot of times. You must remember me! Smith? Soapy Smith? Grayson's. Grayson's best employee?"

Thornhill scrutinized Soapy carefully. "The face is familiar, but I can't say I remember—"

"He's a little hard to forget," Santos suggested, smothering a grin.

"Right," Thornhill agreed. "Well, Mr. Soapy Smith, Grayson's best employee, we'll drop by Grayson's tonight at, say, 11:05. Will that be satisfactory?"

Soapy's "I guess" quavered slightly, but it served the purpose. The three upperclassmen scowled at Soapy, sat back down with the other two girls, and winked at Mitzi as she moved toward another table with Soapy.

"What next?" Soapy moaned. "Mitzi, you've got to save my life."

"That's between you and them, Soapy. Besides, they don't mean anything by it. It's all in fun."

"To heck with that! I mean the entry blank."

"There wasn't anything wrong with the blank, Soapy. I checked it myself."

"But there was, Mitzi. Everything was wrong with it. It was a forgery. Chip didn't sign it!"

"What?"

"Chip didn't sign it!"

"Who did?"

Soapy gulped twice, fast, and confessed: "I signed it."

The rush of words were hard to follow, but Mitzi got the general idea. Soapy held nothing back once he got started. He told her how silly Chip thought the tournament was and how upset he was about the Blond Bomber reference.

Soapy also told her that he hadn't meant to sign Chip's name, but he'd wanted to please her and especially wanted to cheer Chip up and get him back to his old self so that he'd want to play basketball once Dr. Terring cleared him. And he was stupid, and he'd probably lost the best friend of his whole life, and he wished he'd never even heard about this stupid shooting tournament. And Mitzi Savrill, too, he added under his breath.

"*This* is serious, Soapy," Mitzi said gravely. "It isn't only you and Chip involved in this. It's me, and the ethics of newspaper reporting, and a lot of other things. Soapy, why did you ever do such a thing?"

Soapy shook his head mournfully. "Mitzi, I never imagined you'd get into any trouble because of the entry form. Chip would never do anything to hurt you. No one would. What are we gonna do now?"

Mitzi didn't answer. Her agile mind was busy seeking a solution to Soapy's confession. There wasn't any! The entry was a phony. The only person who could straighten out the mess was Chip Hilton.

"What time is it?" she asked.

"One-thirty."

Mitzi headed for a phone booth, talking over her shoulder. "Excuse me, Soapy. I'll be right back. Wait here!"

In three minutes, she was back. "Come on!" she commanded. "We've got to hurry."

Chip Hilton was sitting in the reception office of the *Herald* at that very moment, waiting for Bill Bell, the sports editor, to return from lunch. While he waited, Chip tried to get as much information as possible from the receptionist about the AAU Marksmanship Contest.

"Well, the *Herald* has sponsored the event for several years. The idea was Mr. Bell's. The first year was just for local elementary and middle schoolers, but the event was such a success that it expanded over the years to include entrants from high schools, colleges, and amateur organizations. Then the AAU heard about how successful the idea had been here, and today it's a national event."

"Seems kind of silly for athletes from all over to compete just by shooting a basketball," Chip objected.

"Oh, I don't know. Lots of people seem to think—oh, there's Mr. Bell. He'll see you in just a second. I'll come back for you."

The receptionist followed the tall, graying man into his office and carefully closed the door.

"Mr. Bell," she said, "the young man waiting to see you is Chip Hilton. He wants to talk to you about the shooting tournament. He seems upset about something.

And Mitzi Savrill just called and asked me to tell you that she's on her way and hopes you'll entertain your visitor until she arrives and can explain everything."

"Sounds rather convoluted to me," Bell said, smiling. "Well, whatever Mitzi Savrill says is good enough for me. Besides, I've been wanting to talk to him ever since the football season."

Chip had been a Bill Bell fan from the first day he arrived on campus. He liked the big man very much. Not only because Bell had seemed to understand the Booster situation during those hectic football days, but also because the sports editor was a fine writer. Chip often dreamed of becoming a sportswriter himself.

"Thanks, Mr. Bell. I'm glad to meet you. I won't take much of your time—"

"Time? Hold it a minute, son." Bell smiled and asked Chip to pull his chair up by the desk.

Then Bell studied the freshman through smiling eyes. He liked the close-up of this tall, broad-shouldered athlete. A writer could create a good story about the mechanics of an athlete's performance from the press box, but to get the real, true story, to do a first-class job, the reporter had to know a person, talk to him, and get his view on things. Bill Bell liked to know the people he wrote about. Perhaps that was one of the reasons he was such a great writer.

Bell continued slowly and thoughtfully. "Look, Chip, you're news. Or didn't you realize that the best quarterback we've seen at State for many years was news? I seem to remember there was another guy who came to State a few years before you were born who was news. I had the privilege of being a classmate of his." Bell's thoughts flew back through the years to the father of this quarterback. What an athlete that man had been!

CHIP SEES THE LIGHT

"Your father was probably the greatest we ever had here, Chip. Don't ever get the idea you're riding on his reputation or that just because he happened to be your dad and a great star, good enough to be an all-American in three sports, that you should try to keep your identity unknown—that you can't make good on your own."

Chip interrupted him. "You've got it wrong, Mr. Bell. I never meant to give you that impression."

"I'm glad to hear you say that. You see, I've got a pretty good file here on William 'Chip' Hilton Jr., who stars in football and dabbles a bit in basketball and baseball. I know a lot about him, besides knowing that he's got a pretty good head as a substitute coach, guiding teams to upsets and all that." Bell was smiling again, trying to bring a little humor into the conversation.

"No, Chip, you'll take a lot of time and a lot of space from sportswriters like me in the next three years. Whether you like it or don't like it. You see, Chip, once an athlete—male or female—emerges above the others in his or her particular group, well, that athlete becomes a sort of target for everybody. The jealous try to knock him down; the weak curry his favors as long as he runs at the head of the pack. The outsiders analyze him and try to use him if they can." Bell smiled wryly.

"They're people like me, although I don't exactly see myself as an outsider, because athletes like you are my lifeblood. You provide the material for my stories and, indirectly, allow me to participate in the impact you make on others' lives.

"But I want to get back to you. There are other strong people in your particular sphere, and they will proffer you their respect and friendship. This is the reason you can't shrink back. These people are counting on you. They are proud of you and your accomplishments. Proud of you for developing and utilizing your God-given talents. That's why you and student athletes like you can't perform an outstanding feat that makes news and then hide behind a tree. So don't say anything to me about taking too much of my time. All right?"

Chip nodded. He'd gotten a lot of good out of that little talk. And to think, he'd been considering not playing basketball—that is, if he ever got that crummy medical clearance!

Feeling troubled about his mom and especially discouraged about Red and Soapy not making it, he'd leaned toward just waiting until next year. Everything would be so much simpler next year. He'd been feeling sorry for himself. But now he thought he understood why it was so important to his friends, especially Soapy, that he play. Chip was glad he had come, even if it was about that contest business, which brought him back to the purpose of his visit.

"Thanks, Mr. Bell. I came to talk to you about the basketball shooting tournament. Someone entered me in the contest without me knowing about it. I don't know why, and I don't like the idea."

"Why don't you like the idea, Chip?"

"Well, it seems like showing off. It doesn't prove anything."

Bill Bell nodded. "I guess that's one way of looking at it, Chip, but I don't think it's the right way. Let me ask you a few questions.

"Do you feel all team competition should be restricted to personal contact games? Or that individual contests should be limited to boxing and wrestling? Do you feel that playing tennis or golf or doing tae kwon do is showing off, or that participating in a swim meet or a diving championship is a waste of time?

CHIP SEES THE LIGHT

"How about track and field? Athletes travel all over the world because they excel in throwing the javelin or the discus or the shot or because they jump higher and farther or run faster than someone else. Does that mean that each of those outstanding performers is thinking in terms of showing off?"

Bill Bell leaned back in his chair and regarded Chip quizzically. "What about national teams or the Olympics and all the skill events it encompasses?"

Chip was confused. He knew what the sage sports editor was getting at, and he knew he'd been thrown for a loss. He had been wrong on many levels.

"You win, Mr. Bell," he said, smiling. "I guess you think I'm pretty self-centered."

"No, not at all. But I do think you had the wrong slant on something that makes millions of people happy. Another thing, Chip, about this and what we were talking about before, there's an old saying that's applicable here, right now. It applies to you and this show-off phobia of yours. 'Don't hide your light under a bushel.' Got it?"

Chip stood up and extended his hand. "Thank you, Mr. Bell. I get it more than you know. I sure appreciate everything you said."

"You're entirely welcome, Chip. Excuse me. Yes, Mrs. Radice? Oh, Mitzi. Send her in."

Mitzi entered briskly, happy to have reached the office in time. She breathed a sigh of relief and cast a quick look at Chip. Soapy followed, apprehensive and nervous, his eyes searching Chip's face.

"I gather you know Chip," Bell said.

"Oh yes, very well. This is Soapy Smith. Soapy, this is Mr. Bell."

Soapy advanced warily and extended his hand. "How do you do, sir. Great to meet you."

Chip was puzzled and looked from Mitzi to Soapy, Soapy to Mitzi, trying to figure out what was going on and how to excuse himself from the room. "I'd better be going," he said.

"Oh no, Chip," Mitzi said quickly. "We want you to hear about—"

"About the shooting tournament," Soapy interrupted nervously. "We—er, no—I—"

Bill Bell took charge and stepped cleverly into the breach. "Oh, the entry form. That's all settled, isn't it, Chip?"

Mitzi and Soapy, open-mouthed, swung around to face Chip with astonished eyes.

Chip nodded. "It sure is," he said decisively. "I don't know who entered me in the contest, but he sure did me a big favor."

Soapy nearly jumped out of his skin. "He did?" he cried. "All right! I did!"

CHAPTER 9

Trials, Tribulations, and Tricks

EARLY THE next morning, Chip Hilton's world came crashing down around him like the walls of Jericho. The morning had begun like any other. As always, Soapy's radio alarm clock had launched Chip and Soapy to their feet. Then Soapy, trailing his red and blue State University towel and singing off-key to the radio, had headed out the door for the showers, only to pivot as Chip answered the ringing phone.

No. Nothing suggested that today would be any different. There was nothing to prepare Chip for this sudden call from Doc Jones in Valley Falls. Nothing could have prepared him. Sad memories of his childhood began haunting him again. Only this time, it was his mom.

Doc Jones would tell Chip only that his mom was in Valley Falls Memorial Hospital. John Schroeder, Chip's former boss at the Sugar Bowl, was already on his way to pick Chip up and drive him home to Valley Falls. Doc Jones would explain everything then.

BACKBOARD FEVER

Chip reached for the phone to call Coach Rockwell while Soapy quietly moved through the hall, gathering Chip's lifelong friends. Moments later, Chip mechanically stuffed the clothes Soapy handed him into a small suitcase. Speed and Biggie gathered Chip's books, and Joel and Red called his professors.

They were all running on automatic; the moment was suspended and frozen in time. Years ago, these same friends had been there when Chip had learned about his father's accident, and they were all here again. Back in Valley Falls, the woman they'd all grown to love as a second mom was facing a yet-unnamed battle.

These five friends—Christian and Jew—had not prayed together since they were little boys. But this morning, they solemnly bowed their heads in unison . . . and then Chip was gone.

Brody "Bitsy" Reardon stood five feet, five inches and weighed 135 pounds in his heaviest jersey and pants and holding the ball. But the freshman flash had an eye for the basket. He could shoot a ball through the hoop from nearly any spot on the floor as easily as most people find their mouths with a spoon. He could hit a teammate with a pass when it didn't even look as if he was open, and he could dribble the ball so confidently it sounded like a drummer. On defense, man-to-man, or zone, Bitsy was energy personified! He was just what Henry Rockwell had ordered when it came to the veteran mentor's idea of a point guard, and Reardon was Mr. Hustle on defense. Bitsy had clinched Rockwell's number-one position, the team's quarterback, almost as quickly as he had snatched the first rebound of the season.

Bitsy had other talents. He was graced with a sharp tongue and a quick wit. He was at his best when he had a target for some good-natured razzing. Most afternoons, he kept things lively and the squad laughing, with the exception of the target of his slicing wit.

This afternoon, Bitsy had plenty to say, most of which he'd gleaned from the Sunday *Herald's* report of the alumni game. With the exception of Nick Hunter and Rodney Early, Bitsy had an appreciative and eager audience. Sky Bollinger had antagonized more than one of the freshman players because of his arrogant manner and unblushing self-worship.

Purposefully tardy, wanting his teammates all to be present, Bitsy started as soon as he hit the locker room. "This game of basketball's getting out of hand! First thing you know, the little man will be dominating the game. Any of you guys see what that little Barker kid did the other night? Picked himself up thirty-nine points against some of the best basketball players in this part of the country—if you believe what they say. And, of course, if you've got time to listen to them.

"Biology prof said this morning there were fifteen thousand men in the United States who were six-six or taller and that humans the world over would all someday be giants. He said we wouldn't have to worry about a thing four or five thousand years from now. Anybody interested in doin' a Rip Van Winkle for a few years?

"You guys know what's wrong with basketball? Defense! The Rock's always talking about defense, isn't he? Well, he's wrong too. If he was smart, he'd just eliminate defense altogether and concentrate on shooting. *Imagine!* Here we are with the best shooter in America in our midst, and the coach won't let him do all the shooting! It just isn't fair!

"A real smart coach would make four of us play defense and then put this shooting champion down at the other end of the floor to rest until us, the four other guys, got the ball for him. Wonder how come the coach hasn't thought of that?

"The Rock gave a speech at our sports banquet last year, and he told a story about how they played basketball in his daddy's day. He said they had a center who jumped, and a standing guard who stood, and a running guard who ran and gave the ball to the feeding forward, who fed the ball to the shooting forward, who shot all the baskets (and all the fouls!) and was captain of the team and president of his class and married to the banker's daughter and got to be governor and thought he should've been president of the country and—what's more important—got all the write-ups!

"You guys think we could ever dig up someone like that?

"If I was tall, say six-eight, *maybe* six-nine, and I was playing against a guy, say five-eight, you know what I'd do?"

Sky Bollinger slammed his locker shut and walked over to the bench where Bitsy was lacing up his shoes. Towering over his tiny tormentor, Sky glared down at him with irate indignation.

"No," Bollinger snarled. "What *would* you do, squirt?"

Bitsy leisurely finished lacing his shoes and then spun his body around to the other side of the bench. "Take my ball and go home," he said, leaping to his feet and dancing as far as the door. Then, just before he trotted away, he added, "Then I'd tell my daddy! Gotta practice now. See ya!"

Rockwell didn't hear Bitsy Reardon's monologue, but he was just desperate enough to try anything. Bollinger dogged it on the defense and hogged it on the offense and played "cherry picker" basketball every chance he got. But the first game was only several days away, and the harried mentor decided to go along with the "problem child" and see if there would be a change when the team got into its schedule. The Rock was hoping Sky would prove to be a clutch player. Some athletes can't do a thing in practice but are killers once a game is underway. They play for keeps. Conversely, some athletes can't miss in practice but flop when the pressure is on. In Bollinger's case, it wasn't that he didn't deliver in practice, rather it was that he didn't even try to deliver.

Rockwell gave the squad a stiff workout and then ordered them to the bleachers. "Men," he said, "we've been working pretty hard. But we're far from being ready for our opening game. It isn't your ability or your physical conditioning that disturbs me; it's the almost complete absence of team spirit. I wish you could have heard the talk Coach Ralston gave the freshman football team at Camp Sundown last August. I think I remember the important part, and I'd like to repeat a little of what he said.

"First, Ralston said that a winning team had to have good players. That they had to be fast, aggressive, and smart. He said that first-class physical condition and a mastery of the offensive and defensive skills were necessary. Also, a team that hustled and put out *all* the time was a hard team to beat, but that all those qualities and abilities were insufficient unless *every* player, every player, as an individual and as a member of the team, had that winning spirit.

"I don't think anyone can improve on this part of his speech. At least, I can't. He said, 'Spirit is the thing! School spirit, team spirit, and loyalty to the spirit of the game. Without spirit, no team will ever, can ever, be a great team!'

"I wish all of you would take the essence of those words home with you and think about them. Take my word for it—all you need is the right kind of spirit. Good night, boys."

There wasn't much clowning around in the locker room that night. Athletes get to know one another pretty well when they're practicing, working, and sweating for a common goal. The words had struck home.

But Rockwell hadn't reached Sky Bollinger's heart. Back in the locker room, Sky looked around at the serious faces of his teammates and snickered sardonically. "Don't tell me you hicks are falling for that old, corny rah-rah stuff? You mean you wanna die for dear old State? Hah! Don't forget your pink blankies and pacifiers tomorrow afternoon."

Speed Morris, intensely loyal to his coach, slammed his locker. More than anyone, other than his father, he admired and respected Henry Rockwell, and Sky Bollinger's cutting sarcasm hurt Speed as much as it would have hurt Rockwell. Even more than that, Speed was fearful for Mary Hilton and sick at heart for his best friend, who was a better athlete—even hurt—than Sky Bollinger could ever be. Morris was a good basketball player, too. But he was put at a disadvantage because of his size. He had demonstrated that he was first-string material because of his drive, his defensive play, and his team play. So far, he had gotten the call on sheer ability. Speed expected no breaks from the Rock. In fact, he knew he would have to be head and shoulders above his nearest rival in order to get the nod for the first five.

Morris and Bitsy Reardon were both aware that Sky Bollinger had to be the team's first-class big man and shoulder a big man's responsibilities, or Rockwell would have more than a height problem. Coach would have to sacrifice speed and scoring ability for height and backboard strength.

In the long silence that followed Sky's biting remark, many things crossed Speed's mind. If he challenged Sky's hurtful remarks, it could mean trouble. Sky Bollinger was shallow enough to think Speed's loyalty was just a thinly veiled attempt to make the starting team. But Speed was burning. He had listened to Bollinger cut down the Rock too often.

"Why don't *you* grow up, Bollinger?" Speed said, his voice filled with disgust. "Grow up and start playing instead of talking a good game."

Bollinger was taken by surprise. He wasn't used to anyone calling his bravado. "So," he hissed, "True-Blue Morris is gonna make a loyalty play for a spot as a starter. How about that?" His voice hardened as he continued. "Morris, you stay out of my face, or you'll run into trouble. Right, Nick? Right, Rodney?"

"You got it, Sky!" Nick Hunter growled.

"You tell him, Sky!" Rodney Early added, glaring at Morris.

Speed moved deliberately to the middle of the room. He was fed up now. "You're a coward, Bollinger," he said contemptuously. "You've got a mouth and a streak up your back as wide as this room. Why don't you and your friends just grow up!"

Bollinger didn't move, but Nick Hunter and Rodney Early decided to put Speed in his place. They charged as though they meant to take Speed apart. Only they ran into a surprise. Speed didn't wait.

He met Hunter flush in the mouth with a hard right and knocked him against the lockers. Early's swing was a roundhouse, and Speed ducked it easily, coming up from under it to catch Rodney with a left to the stomach that brought a grunt and a curse.

Hunter had regained his balance by this time and charged again, flailing his fists. But he hit only the air. Speed was aptly named. He was as fast with his fists as he was with his feet. He ducked and pulled away from the wild swings and then punched Nick with a perfect one-two. But his concentration on Hunter was costly; it enabled Early to get behind Speed. Rodney wrapped his long arms around Speed's neck and wrestled him to the floor.

It all happened so suddenly that their teammates just stared, shocked into inaction by the fury and speed of the attack. Then Rudy Slater and Bitsy Reardon swung into action and closed in on Hunter and Early and pulled them away.

Speed was on his feet in a second, his eyes blazing with fury. "All right, Bollinger," he said savagely. "I'm ready to run into trouble. What are you waiting for? More help from your goon buddies?"

"Well, looks like Rock's talk got you three guys fired up!" Reardon cracked, trying to lighten the heaviness in the room. "Come on, Speed." Bitsy grasped him by the arm and pulled him back to his locker. "Everybody just cut it out." He turned back and addressed the room. "Isn't this just great? And after a talk about spirit and team play like the Rock just gave us! He was so right! We don't even know what the word *spirit* means. This isn't any fun. I don't care whether I play on this team or not!"

"Who cares?" Bollinger groused. "Who *could* play for a guy like him?"

"Better men than you," Speed declared through clenched teeth. "Better in heart and integrity and in basketball too! Chip Hilton would make you look like nothing, and you're twice as big as he is. You think you're such a great shot? You couldn't carry Chip's shoes to practice. You *are* yellow. You quitter!"

Bollinger thought he better do something to save face. He tried to get at Speed, uttering meaningless warnings and swinging his arms. But Rudy Slater and Keith Gibbons restrained him without much exertion, and the show was over. For the time being, at least.

Mr. Bollinger was waiting in the car when Sky came out of the gym and listened keenly to his son's account of the lesson he'd given Speed Morris. "If he was a little bigger, Dad, I would've done more."

"You did exactly right, Sky," his father said, patting him on the knee. "Exactly right."

They drove in silence until Sky noticed they were taking the long way home. "Where you going?" he asked.

"Have to pick up Bobby. At the community center, remember?"

"Aw, no. You mean you're going to pick him up every afternoon?"

"It's your mother's idea, Sky. Anyway, it keeps him away from the playground."

"That reminds me," Sky said. "This Morris guy said Chip Hilton's a great shot—that I couldn't carry his shoes. He must be the one behind that Birdie Byrd Blond Bomber story."

"Hilton again? He certainly gets around. That's the reason I put my foot down about the playground."

Bobby was waiting outside the community center and seemed excited about something. He was bursting to tell someone his good news, but someone who would appreciate what he had to share. He wondered how he could get in touch with Chip.

An opportunity came unexpectedly. Mr. Bollinger wanted to see one of the new movie releases at the mall and hustled Mrs. Bollinger away right after dinner, leaving strict orders for the rest of the Bollingers to hit the books. Sky promptly disappeared, and Melanie quickly discovered that Katherine Kinsmore had her modern history book. That left Bobby alone, and he immediately called Grayson's.

All Grayson's employees knew the policy of not taking personal calls during working hours. When Bobby insisted it was just like a personal emergency, Soapy took the call, worried that it was about Mary Hilton.

"Soapy? It's Bobby. Where's Chip? I've got good news! Me and Chip can practice every afternoon at the community center from three to six. Bill Sparks is crazy about football, and he thinks Chip's the best player in the country. He's the director of the boy's division, and he said we could use a basket in the men's gym. And—"

"Whoa, Bobby. Chip's not here. You'll have to call him in Valley Falls, partner. I'll give you the number."

"That won't work. I'm not allowed to make long distance calls without permission. Can't you just tell him to meet me at th—"

Soapy uncharacteristically lowered his voice. "Bobby, he had to go home for a little while. You want his E-mail address?"

"Sure, that'll work! Wait, I'll get a pencil."

"Forget that," Soapy laughed. "It's not exactly too tough to remember: chiphilton.com."

When Bobby hung up, Soapy felt better. He'd been subdued all evening, thinking of Chip and worrying about Mary Hilton. She was like a second mom to him. But mixed in with all that apprehension was a sense of relief. After days and nights of misery, his conscience was clear. He had told Chip everything. Whatever trials, tribulations, or tricks he might face later in the evening he quickly waved aside as unimportant in the greater scheme of things. Others had lived through these capers or practical jokes or whatever these juniors called them. Besides, maybe he'd get some new ideas.

So, at precisely 11:04, Soapy blew Mitzi a kiss, told Fireball he might not see him again, and walked out the door, surrendering meekly to Don Santos, Kirk Barkley, and Andy Thornhill. The juniors escorted Soapy courteously around the corner and then, with sinister laughs, pushed him into the back seat of a rented black limo. It was like one of those scenes that is supposed to look serious in a bad movie but ends up looking pretty silly. Soapy found himself between two heavy-muscled students, who quickly covered his eyes with a black mask.

Soapy, a victim of watching too many classic mystery movies and reading too many spy novels, tried to keep track of the turns and estimate the distance they were traveling. He counted the number of stops, figuring they were lights, and tried to gauge the speed they were traveling by the sound of the engine. He knew the car had turned off the paved streets as it bumped around the last few minutes of the journey and then came to an abrupt stop. Some late crickets were serenading a bullfrog or two.

Standing in absolute darkness on the uneven, damp ground, Soapy was given a quick and just trial. Did he or did he not disturb a junior class study group during lunchtime? And how did he plead?

"Guilty as charged!" Soapy said stoutly.

Did he or did he not fail to properly address the said study group and/or specific individuals within that study group?

"Guilty, again. You got me," Soapy said simply.

Was he or was he not extremely uncouth in his approach to the entire group?

Soapy thought that one was unfair. "Objection, Your Most Exaltedness. I was wearing a nice shirt, my jeans were clean, I used deodorant, and I even brushed my teeth. Even my socks matched," he said indignantly.

Someone chuckled but quickly covered it up as a cough.

"Better drop that charge, Mr. Exalted," another joked.

There were other charges, but on the whole Soapy thought they were pretty funny. When the questioning ceased, a vote was taken to determine whether Soapy was innocent or guilty. As Soapy expected, there were no votes for his innocence.

"Soapy Smith, Grayson's best employee, you are pronounced worthy of admission to the Mohican Club with special decorations. And, an honorary member of the junior class for seeing the errors of your ways and being a good sport."

Soapy never liked to talk about what happened next. Someone ran an object through the hair on the top of his head, and then he felt hands rubbing something on his hair. Then, he was directed to undress down to his State University boxers. He almost laughed out loud thinking what his dad would say if he was there. Again, he felt hands rub something on his back and arms. He was told to hold out his right hand and smile. Someone put a wooden object in his hand and tied a cloth around his head. Then he heard a click and sensed light for just an instant through the blindfold.

Somehow his inquisitors never discovered the compass Soapy had clutched in his hand ever since he'd left Grayson's. When the laughter stopped, they said good night and good luck and told him they'd deliver his clothes to the dorm.

Soapy grinned to himself. He'd proved once again that the old redhead was a step ahead of most situations. Fortunately, it wasn't too cold, and his only real problem was reading the compass. He'd find a light somewhere.

TRIALS, TRIBULATIONS, AND TRICKS

Soapy found a light all right. At dawn! He was also horrified to find his body was striped with some kind of green Day-Glo paint that seemed to grow brighter when he tried to rub it off with dried leaves. The sun peeked over the mountain about that time. Soapy checked his compass and started south. Shivering and hungry and desperate, Soapy skirted the highway and figured he would soon arrive at Jeff.

But Soapy had made a mistake. He had started south when he should have traveled north. Hungry, tired, cold, and discouraged—and no longer seeing the humor—Soapy finally decided to ask for directions. He knocked on the door of the first farmhouse he saw. The sleepy-eyed man who came to the door was still chuckling over last night's late-night TV show. He had laughed sarcastically at the report about the two Appalachian Trail hikers who had seen a sulphur-breathing monster arrive by meteor from Venus. Then he saw Soapy!

Completely shocked, stunned, and suddenly wide awake, the man screamed, slammed the door, stumbled backward, tripped over his yelping dog, and raced to the phone, yelling, "Call 9-1-1! Call 9-1-1! They're here too!"

As Soapy sprinted past the clothesline, he grabbed a pair of jeans and a sweatshirt and ran toward the treeline.

After what seemed like hours, a driver in a red pickup stopped next to Soapy. A few years earlier, he'd experienced the same kind of "higher education." He drove Soapy all the way to University and to Jefferson Hall. As Soapy opened the door, he hoped he'd find Chip at his computer with his earphones on. But the room was empty and ever so lonely.

CHAPTER 10

Buddy Basketball

EXTRATERRESTRIAL INVASIONS have attracted attention for years. Movies on the big screen and TV series about aliens have continued to draw wide audiences. It shouldn't be surprising that local University papers ran photos of the farmer, his wife, and the yelping dog under the headline "Visitor from Venus", suitably accompanied by an artist's sketch of the alien.

The farmer's testimony was specific, "It was green and it had a phosphorus glow. A green stripe ran across the top of its odd-shaped head and down to the end of its nose. What little hair there was on top of its head was fiery red, and there were tiny red spots all over its face."

The farmer and the dog had been offered a free trip to New York to appear on the "Late Show with David Letterman," the same program he'd been watching the night before the alien stranger had appeared at his back door.

Everyone in Jeff thought it was a good joke, but Soapy didn't agree. He exchanged his regular baseball cap for Biggie Cohen's oversized one after he finally got the paint out of his hair. Then he decided to make the most of his "accident."

"Yes," he assured everyone, "I was lucky! It was a terrible accident! I nearly got myself pulled into the machine! People should never fool around with milkshake machines! They can be dangerous in untrained hands." Word quickly spread about the real story and what a good sport Soapy had been, and his campus notoriety grew. He gave up the baseball cap, got a buzz cut, and enjoyed the additional attention. It was a welcome diversion for his acute apprehension about Chip and Mary Hilton.

The next afternoon in Valley Falls, Chip sat in the dimly-lit hospital chapel, replaying in his mind the events of the previous weeks. The first signs had been small, and Chip realized now he'd missed most of them.

When he and the guys had gone home for Thanksgiving, a thought had registered and then evaporated in the enjoyment of the day: *Gosh, she looks so tiny carrying that platter of turkey.* Later, when he remembered that momentary impression, he'd dismissed it. His mom had always been thin. He figured she looked that way to him because he'd been away at school and just hadn't seen her for a while. And none of the other guys had seemed to notice anything different.

His mom's E-mails to him had been as upbeat as ever, but her voice had sounded tired on the phone the last few times he'd called her—distant and small and vulnerable somehow.

But then, slowly, he started to worry something might really be wrong. His mom had E-mailed him that she was going to see Doc Jones for a physical. "I'm not concerned,

Chip. I'm just a little tired and figure I need some vita-
mins. Maybe I'm missing something zesty in my diet.
Even Hoops is starting to get tired of my leftovers."

He had thought about telling Soapy or Speed about
it, but he just couldn't. What if something was really
wrong with his mom? He didn't think he could go
through that kind of ordeal again.

But her phone call a few days later had truly
alarmed Chip. Doc Jones said she had to undergo some
routine tests—"nothing major, Chip"—but one test
required an overnight stay at the hospital. She'd called
only to let him know where she was in case he called
home. They'd joked about Hoops, the Hilton family cat,
having the run of the house. "Now don't worry, Chip. I'll
be just fine, and I'll be back home tomorrow." And she
was home the next day, and she sounded fine, almost like
her old self.

But she wasn't fine, and three days later their world
had collapsed. Now, Chip knew his mom's overnight hospital stay had been for a biopsy. Three days later, the
results had come back positive: his mom had cancer. And
today the doctors would operate.

Sitting quietly on the edge of the pew, Chip's memories recalled scenes of his childhood when his father was
still alive. *How easy it is to lose sight of our blessings. I
thought I'd learned that lesson with Dad.*

A small tear worked its way down Chip's cheek and
caught at the corner of his lips. He stirred himself.
Enough of this! Right now his mother needed his prayers
most of all. But he also realized he'd been right. He
couldn't go through this ordeal again—not alone.

His knees sank to the floor, and his heart turned to
prayer.

BUDDY BASKETBALL

A few nights later at Grayson's, Fireball and Soapy were cleaning up after the pregame crowd. Soapy was feeling great! Chip had called him from the hospital as soon as Mary Hilton had come out of the operating room and was in recovery. She was OK. Since then, he'd called Soapy, Speed, and the other guys several times.

Mary Hilton was in good spirits but very tired. Chip spent several hours at the hospital each day, keeping her company. Mary Hilton's physician was a cancer specialist who was highly recommended by Doc Jones and J. P. Ohlsen. Dr. Marjorie Nader met with Chip and his mom daily, telling them straight out what could lie ahead. She was a wonderful surgeon, and Mary Hilton felt comfortable in her care. They were waiting for important test results that would tell Dr. Nader the next course of action.

Chip was keeping up with his assignments, so college was pretty much under control. He'd also gotten special permission from the dean to have the Hiltons' car on campus when he returned so he could get home every few days. And, of course, he wanted to know how Bobby was doing and asked Soapy to encourage the little guy to keep up his practicing. Yes, Soapy was feeling great!

At 7:15, Fireball clicked on the radio to catch the freshman game on the University station, WSUN 1100. Gerald Gray, WSUN's sports announcer, was broadcasting from the scorer's table at Assembly Hall.

"Good evening, basketball fans. This is Gerald 'Gee Gee' Gray, and welcome to State University basketball! Tonight we're courtside at Assembly Hall and bringing you this first freshman basketball broadcast of the season, courtesy of WSUN 1100 and the State Athletic Association.

BACKBOARD FEVER

"The old backboard fever has gripped yours truly, and the epidemic is spreading every day as the ball that bounces around the world is beginning to pound its way right into the gyms, homes, hearts, and sports pages of the nation.

"This freshman game between State and York Junior College is due to tip-off in just a couple of minutes. Tonight, we meet the newcomers to State basketball. We'll give you all the information on State's starting lineup and the rest of the squad as we get underway, but they're coming out on the floor now. State's new freshman coach, Henry Rockwell, is starting numbers 10, 23, 33, 40, and 55.

"No question about the identity of number 55! Just listen to that crowd! Of course, that's our local favorite, our own Sky Bollinger—looking mighty big and tough and good out there. He's the biggest man on the floor and we think the best on the floor.

"York has also taken the floor for warm-ups. We'll give you their names and numbers in just a moment. Now back to our crew.

"Freshman 33 is Reardon, a little guy who is starting at point guard. Robert 'Speed' Morris is 23, 55 is hometown hero William 'Sky' Bollinger, and 40 is Nick Hunter. Nick needs no introduction to local fans; he played with Bollinger on last year's local high school team. Number 10 is Rudy Slater. Slater is the kid from Cumberland who won outstanding honors here on this very floor last spring.

"Let's run down the York squad: number 21 is Keats, 43 is Cushman, 14 is Markham, 52 is Billings, and 35 is Koenig. The officials look like they're all set. Now, here's our guest soloist this evening, Joyce Cooke, singing 'The Star-Spangled Banner.'"

BUDDY BASKETBALL

Fireball and Soapy glanced at each other and grinned when Speed's name was announced as a starter and he ran onto the court.

"That's a break," Soapy breathed with a wink.

Fireball nodded. "Keep your fingers crossed."

"You think Bollinger and Hunter will freeze him out?"

"Maybe not."

Up in the bleachers in Assembly Hall, Mr. Bollinger, Mrs. Bollinger, Melanie, and Bobby were standing side by side. When the anthem ended and the crowd began to settle in their seats, Mr. Bollinger remained standing, his eyes focused on Sky. Mrs. Bollinger tugged his jacket and pulled him gently down to the bleacher seat. "The people behind us can't see, Bill," she said softly.

Sky Bollinger got the jump and tapped the ball to Hunter. Speed cut around the official and was three feet in front of his man, but he didn't get the ball. Nick ignored Morris and his other teammates completely; he dribbled slowly to the other side of the court and waited until Sky posted up. Then he flipped the ball to his buddy. Bollinger shot almost as soon as he got the ball, wheeling and laying it up with his right hand. But the shot was too hard, the ball carried too much spin, and the York center easily grabbed the rebound.

Rockwell leaned forward and shook his head. His neck muscles bulged, and a wave of red began to color his face. The Rock didn't like buddy basketball.

At the half, the freshmen were leading 32-25. Bollinger had garnered fourteen points for himself. But that was the extent of his contribution on both ends of the court. Speed and Slater were doing all the rebounding, and that eliminated all possibility of the fast break because Bollinger and Hunter refused to run. They preferred the slow setup on offense so that Sky would have a chance to get set under the basket.

Business was slow at Grayson's and Fireball and Soapy exchanged uneasy glances as the game went into the final minutes of the second half. The game had been all Bollinger and Hunter. Speed hadn't scored a point.

"Reardon brings the ball upcourt, dribbling slowly. Hunter is calling for the ball, but the little guard is hanging on to it. He's being pressed now, but he's an excellent ball handler, and the York defenders are not having any luck getting the ball away from him.

"There he goes. Pretty, pretty play. Fans, that was as pretty a play as you'll ever see. Reardon coaxed his guard up close, then passed to Morris, and then cut to the basket—a perfect give-and-go play if there ever was one. Morris hit the speedy point guard just right, and there it was, two quick points. That makes it 51-42.

"York brings the ball upcourt. They're running a screen now with a roll, trying to get the ball in to Billings under the basket. The York pivot man is tricky, about six-five and 185 pounds. There's not much bulk on those bones, but he's beautiful to watch around the basket.

"There's the pass—he has the ball—he scores, and that makes seventeen points he's dropped through the nets. Bollinger has scored twenty.

"Morris takes the rebound on Sky's miss, passes to Reardon, back to Slater, and over to Morris. The flashy guard from Valley Falls passes out to Reardon, and he shoots—nothin' but net from three-point land. Reardon hit from way out on that one, folks; he's done all the scoring in the last few minutes!

"York brings the ball up the court. From Keats over to Cushman, to Koenig, and he holds it. Billings is working for a position under the basket; he's got twenty points now. There's the pass—Billings has it—he fakes a shot—he fakes a drive—he puts up a soft baby-jumper—and it's in! That makes it State 54, York 44.

"Hold it! There's a foul on the play: Bollinger fouled Billings. He's at the line—he bounces the ball—he puts it up—it's good, and the score is now 54-45 and Billings has, let's see, Billings and Bollinger are tied with twenty-three points apiece.

"This game's about over, folks. Rudy Slater takes the ball out of bounds. He passes in to Morris. It's over to Reardon, back to the speedster. That freshman's certainly named right! Morris is dribbling—Bollinger is all set up under the basket—he's waving for the ball. Morris passes to Reardon—the little guard is dribbling now, and Hunter is trying to get the ball. Bitsy's own teammate is trying to take the ball away from him. Must have been a miscommunication on their part. Now, Reardon passes back to Morris. This is beautiful to watch. The freshman back-court duo are putting on a wonderful display, and the score is still 54-45. There's no danger, of course, but the Rock has evidently given orders for the backcourt aces to work the ball around. Morris is watching the clock.

"It looks like he's going to set up Reardon again for a shot. Morris passes the ball out to Reardon. The tiny guard sets—he shoots—there's the horn. The ball is in the air—it looks good—it's in! The official signals two points! His toes were just on the three-point line.

"That winds up this first freshman game, fans. Coach Henry Rockwell's kids are off to a good start. The final score: State Freshmen 56, York 45. We return to wrap everything up after these words from our sponsors."

Mr. Bollinger had been keeping score all through the game, and he nearly died in the second half. "What's the matter with that Morris and Reardon?" he muttered. "What are they trying to do?" He turned abruptly to Mrs. Bollinger. "You see that?" he demanded.

"Really, Bill, I don't know what you're talking about."

"Don't know what I'm talking about! What do you come to these games for, *anyway*? I'm talking about the way those two clowns kept the ball away from Sky. That's what I'm talking about! I'd think you'd be interested in your own son enough to pay attention. Aw, what's the use? Come on. Let's get out of here."

"Aren't you going to wait for Sky?" Mrs. Bollinger asked.

"No," Mr. Bollinger said shortly. "I've got something to do."

Fireball and Soapy discussed the game in between customers and waited eagerly for Speed to drop by. He arrived shortly, and they peppered him with questions.

"What happened?" Soapy demanded.

Speed grinned. "Nothing much. Bitsy and I had a little meeting of the basketball minds about midway through the second half. We decided to play a little buddy basketball ourselves."

"What happened after the game?"

"Nothing much. Bollinger and his crew were pretty hot, but Rudy Slater, Keith Gibbons, and Bitsy stuck with me in the locker room. We let the three must-get-theirs know there wasn't gonna be any buddy basketball stuff."

Soapy breathed a sigh of relief. "I'm worried about that bunch, Speed. You be careful."

Henry Rockwell was far from satisfied with the game. He recognized York for just what it was, a one-man team. That disturbed him most. York's pivot man, who was inches shorter, had clearly outplayed Bollinger. The points meant nothing. It was the rebounding, the passes, the points in the paint, and the outlet passes for the transition that made Bollinger look pale in comparison. "He'll never stand up against a man anywhere near his size," he mused. "And he's gonna ruin some fine ballplayers."

Rockwell was no fool. He was perfectly aware of the rupture between Bollinger, Hunter, and Early on one side and Morris and Bitsy Reardon on the other. But despite the seriousness of the situation, he had gotten a kick out of the freezing lesson Morris and Reardon had given Bollinger and Hunter. Not that he approved it, but it struck a sympathetic chord.

The varsity got off to a good start, too, defeating Southeastern 72-63. After the game, Rockwell and Corrigan walked home, stopping for a cup of coffee on the way.

"Not so good, Rock?"

Rockwell shook his head. "Nope," he said wryly. "It sure isn't."

There was a short pause. Then Rockwell continued. "You know, Jim, this whole thing could be worked out if only Chip Hilton were able to play. He's six-four and an excellent shot, a real team player. He's just what I need to bring Bollinger and a few others to their senses. He's made real progress with the physical therapy work Mike Terring set up, but now with his mom's illness, I just don't know. It's tough. I know he wants to be out there."

Corrigan reached across the table and laid his hand on the older man's arm. "Look, Rock," he said warmly, "I want you to know something. We all appreciate what you're doing for the program. You're a great guy. I mean it with all my heart. Whatever you do about Sky

Bollinger is all right with Dad and especially with me. I'd like to see him make good, of course. It would mean two or three great years for the school and for me, and I could sure use a couple. But there's a limit to everything. Just keep in mind that you're among friends. We think you're tops, and we'll stick with you if we never win a game!"

There wasn't much Rockwell could say to that, but the crooked smile, which crept across his lips, and the sudden warmth that filled his steady black eyes expressed a lot.

Corrigan felt pretty good after he left Rockwell. A person always feels good when he knows he's created a bond of friendship with someone he admires. Jim stepped out with long, happy strides that soon brought him to his home . . . and a visitor.

William Bollinger Sr. opened the door of his car and stepped directly in Corrigan's path. Jim was startled for a moment, but when he recognized the man, his jaw hardened.

"Hello, Coach. Congratulations. Nice victory."

"Thanks, Mr. Bollinger. It was a start."

"Got a minute?"

"Guess so. It's pretty late though."

"I won't keep you long; I just wanted to talk to you about Sky and this new coach, Rockwell."

"What's on your mind, Mr. Bollinger?"

"Call me Bill. Well, clearly, this Rockwell isn't using Sky right. I watched that game pretty close tonight, and it looks to me like Rockwell is playing politics and using favorites."

"I don't follow you."

"Well, he's using one of his old high school players, Morris, to team up with Reardon to keep the ball away from Sky. My son has had a little trouble with those two, and I was watching them all through the game. I saw everything with my own eyes. Why, Sky should've had forty points against the guy he was matched with tonight."

Corrigan was thankful for the darkness so Bollinger couldn't see the feelings of irritation on his face. He took a deep breath and relaxed with difficulty. "That might be," he said thoughtfully. "But there's a lot more to basketball than scoring. After all, this wasn't a very high scoring game. Let's see, the score was 56-45. How many points did Sky get?"

"Only twenty-three!"

"That's nearly half of his team's total, Mr. Bollinger. I'd say that was pretty good."

Corrigan grasped Bollinger's arm in a firm grip. "Why don't you just sit back for a couple of weeks and let this problem work itself out? I bet you'll get a kick out of Sky working out his own problems."

Standing on the porch a few seconds later, Corrigan watched Bollinger drive away. "And I hope you do," he breathed angrily. "A kick right in the seat of the pants!"

CHAPTER 11

A Lot at Stake

CHIP TIPTOED into the room and stood quietly at the foot of his mom's hospital bed. She was asleep. The late afternoon sun filtered through the blinds and brightened the yellow tint of her hair to a burnished gold. Chip's heart filled with all the love he felt for his mom and also all the tension of these weeks. Sensing her son's presence, she stirred and smiled, the first real smile he'd seen in what seemed a lifetime.

The latest lab results confirmed Dr. Nader had gotten all the cancer. His mom would have to stay in the hospital at least a week, but she should be home for Christmas.

The entire room was filled with flowers from friends in Valley Falls. As Chip leaned over to kiss his mom's forehead, he caught sight of the large poinsettia on the table.

Mary Hilton smiled. "It arrived today. Beautiful, isn't it? Mitzi must be quite a girl." Chip blushed and stammered a little, and his mom enjoyed every second. "Oh, and there's a huge box of candy from Soapy. He said I needed some fattening up," she laughed.

After much discussion, they decided Chip would return to State at least until his mom was released from the hospital. He could meet with his professors to reschedule his final exams, work a few hours at Grayson's, and get checked out by the team physician. His mom's recovery period would be a month or longer, but Karen Browning, the next-door neighbor, would be able to stay with her whenever she needed, and Chip would come home whenever he could. Suzy Browning would take care of Hoops. It was all set.

That evening, as Chip drove back to State, he was determined to make this holiday season special for as many people as he could. As the time and miles passed, his thoughts turned to Bill Bell and how their conversation had taught him so much and even prepared him to deal with his mom's crisis. Then his thoughts shifted to Bobby and how he was coming along with his shooting.

Bill Bell had been a basketball fan and true student of the game for years. He liked basketball because anyone, anywhere, indoors or outdoors, male or female, young or old, tall or short, could play the game. He relished the history of the game, from its early beginnings in 1891, using Dr. James Naismith's original thirteen rules at the Springfield, Massachusetts, YMCA, to its worldwide acceptance at every level. Even though contemporary players were certainly more skilled, Bell believed they knew less about the game than in the "old days" when players knew more about the game's origin and development. The *Herald*'s veteran sportswriter decided to do something about it. The result was the formation of the National Basketball Marksmanship Tournament. From a humble start in the local community center, the idea had grown and developed until it attracted the attention of the AAU and won the sponsorship of that powerful organization.

Bell had originally selected and defined the shots, and it was a credit to his knowledge of basketball that the original ten shots remained the basic test. The AAU issued a leaflet defining the shots and containing other information regarding tournament procedure. Chip and Bobby knew the rules by heart, and they followed them to the letter in practicing the championship routine. With only a few days remaining before the opening shots of the tournament, they were hard at practice in the community center gym.

"Let's do it again, Bobby," Chip said. "Right from the beginning. Just the way you're going to do it Saturday morning when you win the district championship. I'll call them and read the rules. All set?"

Bobby nodded, then dribbled in for a layup from the right side of the basket with his right hand. He followed with the same shot from the left side with his left hand. The ball wobbled but dropped through, and they both cheered. Then Bobby dribbled down the center and took off with a perfect one-two stride and laid the ball over the top of the basket and against the backboard for another score. It was a hard shot for Bobby when the ten-foot basket was used. Chip smiled and nodded his head in satisfaction. "Good! Now the cut shots!"

After the cut shots, both banked, left and right, Chip called for the tap-in shot. "This is the tough one, Bobby. Good thing for you they use eight-foot baskets for your division."

Bobby grinned. "I still can't do it."

"You've got to try."

While Chip had been in Valley Falls, Dickie had fallen far behind Bobby, grown discouraged, and decided to give up on the tournament. Not Bobby! He had grown more determined than ever. Maybe Dickie gave up so easily because, unlike Bobby, he didn't have the challenge of an older brother who dominated the entire family. There was a lot at stake for Bobby.

The tournament rules required that using only the right hand, the ball be tapped from the right up against the backboard and then into the basket; the shot was then repeated from the left side using the left hand. Chip excelled in this drill because of his exceptional coordination, his ability to leap, tap the ball in the basket with his right hand, land on the floor, and then leap and tap the ball into the basket with his left hand.

Bobby went right on through the pivot shots, the floating shot, the one-hand running shot, the one-hand set, the two-hand set, the two-hand overhead, the dribble stop and jump, and finally the free throw. In the free throw competition, the contestant was required to attempt three types of shots, the one-hand set, the two-hand set, and the underhand lift shot. These old-fashioned shots were completely new skills for most of the entrants and required lots of practice.

Bobby had improved so much that Chip had strong hopes for his young pal. When he finished, Bobby retrieved the ball, and they went through the list again with Chip doing the shooting. Chip seldom missed, and Bobby's eyes expressed his admiration. "Man, Chip," he breathed, "you just can't miss! You do 'em all good. Sky can't do the floating or the running or the jump shots very good, and he can't shoot a free throw any way except with one hand. He's not very good with a two-hand set, either."

Chip still wasn't satisfied. "We'll go through it once more," he said.

At 5:30 they called it a day. Chip headed off to Jeff to call his mom and have dinner before starting work at Grayson's, and Bobby waited in front of the building for his father to pick him up. Bobby was thrilled through and through. He was thinking of nothing except the Saturday morning qualifying rounds.

In the car, coming from Assembly Hall, Mr. Bollinger was sounding off as usual about Coach Rockwell. "I talked to Corrigan, and I think I'll have to have another session with this Rockwell. You stick it out for two or three more games, and then we'll see. The big deal right now, Sky, is the shooting tournament. You haven't been practicing, and after me spending all that money for the glass board."

"Don't you start on me too. Taking Rockwell's guff for an hour is enough for one day."

"I'm just trying to tell you how important it is to be in good shape for the nationals, Sky," Mr. Bollinger placated. "There's Bobby! On time for once."

"It's three weeks off," Sky grumbled. "I'm not worried about my shooting, but I am worried about Bobby and the disgrace he's going to bring to the whole family. You gonna let him go through with this?"

"The shooting tournament? You know I can't do anything about it now, Sky. Your mother would hit the ceiling! I don't know what's gotten into her all of a sudden."

Mr. Bollinger pulled over to the curb, and Bobby climbed into the back seat. Neither his father nor his brother greeted him or asked him about school or his practice. They were too self-centered. Bobby was used to the treatment. He got it all the time. But he was man enough to say hello and to ask Sky how practice had been. Sky's only answer was a contemptuous snort. They rode in silence the rest of the way, and Bobby was glad to escape from the car.

Chip was elated after calling his mom. She'd been released from the hospital that morning, and Karen Browning was staying with her until he came home. When Chip arrived at Grayson's, everybody was buzzing about the big Christmas dance that night at the University Hotel and Convention Center. Soapy was waiting for him in the employee lounge area, scrubbed till he shone and wearing his best blue suit. Fireball was a sight, too, in patent leather shoes and a black tuxedo. He grinned sheepishly when Chip looked him up and down.

"Heavy date, Chipper," he said, explaining the tux. "First time in my life I ever had to drag excess baggage to a dance."

Soapy leaped to his feet. "Excess baggage! Who asked her first? Who you trying to kid? She's my date! We're letting you go along because you couldn't get a date for yourself. Besides, Chip's going with us too."

Fireball laughed. "All right, handsome," he said, "you win! You asked her first and that's that. We'll just wait and see who has the last dance."

Chip wasn't as easily pacified. "What did you say, Soapy?"

"I merely said you're going to the dance too."

"That's what you think!"

"No, Chipper, my beloved pal, that's what Mitzi thinks."

Soapy was right. Mitzi had a few words with Chip. To no one's surprise, he was ready to go at 11:15 that evening. Five minutes later, Mitzi, devastatingly beautiful in a black evening gown and accompanied by two ardent

escorts and a reluctant one, left Grayson's. George
Grayson himself was on hand to open the door of the car
and wished them a happy evening.

When the foursome entered the ballroom at the
hotel, it was like going outdoors following a snowstorm.
The motif was winter with festive decorations for the holiday season. There was white cotton for the background
effects, other decorations of holly, evergreen, green and
white serpentine, and balloons of all colors floated here
and there, hovering near the ceiling.

The dance was well underway when they arrived,
but the Grayson foursome's entrance was startling
enough to attract a lot of comment and attention. Not
because of the devoted attention of the athletic escorts,
but because Mitzi was easily the most eye-catching coed
in the room. Fireball and Soapy were as proud as pea-
cocks, but it was Chip who led her onto the floor.

During the rest of the evening, hundreds of eyes
watched the quartet with mixed emotions. The boys
watched because they couldn't break through the three-
man defense. The girls watched because of Mitzi's over-
abundance of escorts. Who had ever heard of a girl coming to a dance with three guys? Especially three
freshmen athletes whose names were already becoming
bywords on the campus?

Mitzi loved to dance and had a way of making her
partner feel he was the best dancer on the floor. Strange
as it may seem, none of the three escorts made an effort
to dance with any of the other girls, and this was as
much a surprise as their original entrance. Mitzi was
happy to dance with her three coworkers, and they were
satisfied to sit out the extra dances.

Chip enjoyed the evening almost as much as Soapy
and Fireball. When the band announced the last dance,

A LOT AT STAKE

Mitzi took advantage of the verbal sparring match between Soapy and Fireball to pull Chip onto the floor, ending the sideline struggle. Soapy and Fireball looked at each other mournfully, solemnly shook hands, and glumly waited for Mitzi and Chip to rejoin them.

They brightened up later when they stopped at a restaurant near the campus. The rivals took over then for the benefit of the spectators and swung into their regular kidding routine. Then, to the amusement of the same customers, all three boys escorted Mitzi home.

Jeff was a busy place the next day. Students were checking out all day, going home for the holidays, and by six o'clock, Chip, Soapy, Speed, and Pete Randolph were the only residents left. Biggie Cohen, Red Schwartz, Joel Ohlsen, and Tug Rankin were the last to leave and said they would be listening to the broadcast of the shooting tournament and the freshman game.

Chip went to bed thinking first about his mom and then about the tournament, and before he realized it could be possible, he was sitting beside Speed and Soapy in the senior section of the bleachers. There were four classes: twelve and under, intermediate, junior, and senior. Bobby's class was first on the program.

"Where did all these people come from?" Soapy gasped. "They're crazy!"

"They're all from this section of the state," Chip explained. "If all these people are here for the first age group, the gym will be packed this afternoon."

Chip wasn't interested in the crowd. He was trying to locate Bobby. There were four baskets roped off and restricted to the contestants and judges. Each contestant was numbered for one of the four baskets. The names were called in groups of four, and each contestant's successes and misses were recorded. Only two competitors could win in each class. The morning rounds were to determine the qualifying competitors from the local section for the state championships to be held that afternoon. The national championships were scheduled for Saturday, January 11.

Chip looked for Bobby in the section of bleachers roped off for the twelve and under contestants, but there were a few hundred kids in the group. "To heck with the rules," he muttered, rising and starting down the aisle.

"What'd you say?" Soapy asked. "Where you going?"

"I said forget the rules. Wait here. I'll be right back."

Bobby saw Chip first. "Hey, Chip! Up here!"

Seconds later Chip was sitting beside his friend. "Where's your family?"

"They—they couldn't come," Bobby said evasively. "My mom said she'd try to get here this afternoon."

"Good," Chip said cheerfully. "How do you feel? Confident? Feel as though you can knock down a hundred in a row? Good! Now I'm going to sit right here until you win. You just go up there and shoot the way you've been shooting at the community center, OK?"

Bobby swallowed nervously and nodded, but Chip could see that his buddy had the fever, all right. Stage fright on the court! He patted the little guy on the back. Then he did it again. "Look, Bobby," he said firmly, "we've been practicing and hoping for this a long time. There's a lot at stake. You know what I mean."

Bobby knew. When his name was called a few minutes later, he was his old self, eager and determined.

Chip sat there just like a parent or a coach, his heart filled with emotion, pulling for Bobby with everything he had. Where was the kid's family? At least Sky, anyway. There wasn't much excuse for him. He didn't have anything to do until the freshman game tonight. If the little shooter could only get by this morning.

He watched Bobby take his practice shots, wondering if the eight-foot basket would throw him off. The young hoopster was on his own now, that was for sure.

Bobby bounced the ball a couple times to get the feel of it and took his warm-up shots. Then an official, clipboard in hand, gave him the go-ahead sign.

The layups and the cut shots were easy for Bobby, and Chip glowed with pride at his confidence. But he closed his eyes when Bobby got to the distance shots. After a full minute he looked down once again, and what he saw encouraged him. Bobby was on target! Chip felt proud, and a choking feeling gripped his throat. A few minutes later, Bobby finished with the free throws and bounded up the aisle to Chip's side.

"Nice going, Bobby," Chip said, shaking hands. "You were great. It's going to take a champ to beat that score. Did they tell you how you made out?"

"No," Bobby said happily. "They just said we'd have to wait until one o'clock for the announcement. The man keepin' my score said I was the best he'd had so far though. You know, Chip, if—"

Chip nodded. "I know. Guess I'd better get back where I belong. Are you going home for lunch?"

"I won't have time if I win. I have to shoot again at two o'clock."

"Good. We'll have lunch together no matter how we come out. You won't mind if Speed and Soapy—"

Bobby beamed. "Mind?"

Chip found a newcomer sitting in his seat when he returned. Speed introduced him. "This is Bitsy Reardon, Chip. Bitsy's the point guard I was telling you about. Remember?"

"I sure do! Good luck, Bitsy."

"I haven't got a chance," Reardon said. "This was Coach Rockwell's idea. From what Speed tells me about you, I sure wish the all-American was shooting this afternoon."

"Man, the great Bollinger doesn't have to compete until the nationals," Speed chided. "How many times does *he* have to tell you he's the national champion?"

"My mistake," Reardon said. "How could I forget anything the wizard of roundball told me?"

The announcer interrupted them, calling the senior competitors. "Brown, Denton, Hilton, and Williams, report to your respective baskets."

"Good luck, Chipper," Speed said, gripping his friend's arm.

"All the best, Hilton," Reardon added.

"He'll kill 'em!" Soapy declared loudly, glaring fiercely at the other competitors.

Chip did just that. His score was as nearly perfect as humanly possible, and he received the first crowd cheer of the morning. He waited until Speed and Bitsy had taken their shots, and then the four freshmen found Bobby and went to lunch.

Bobby didn't want to eat, but Chip reminded him that an athlete couldn't be at his best unless he was physically right. At 12:30, Bobby had reached a restless stage that was rapidly turning him into a nervous wreck, and they started back to learn the results. Chip took long strides when he walked, but he and his friends still had a hard time keeping up with Bobby.

They were early, and the judges were late. So they sat side by side on the first row of bleachers and talked nervously. It was 1:15 before the announcer called for attention, and Bill Bell took over.

A LOT AT STAKE

"Ladies and gentlemen, it is my pleasure to announce the winners of the district 8 qualifying tests. These district champions are eligible to compete in the state championships beginning at two o'clock this afternoon."

"Stop stalling and get on with it!" Soapy hissed.

"In the twelve and under class, the number-one position goes to Stefan Sadokierski."

A group of kids from the suburb of Wellsville leaped to their feet, stomped the bleachers, and cheered wildly for their state hopeful. Bell, smiling, held up his hand as he continued.

"The number-two winner is Robert Bollinger of the University Community Center."

Bobby didn't move. He just sat there, pressing his hands together in his lap. Chip, Speed, Soapy, and Bitsy brought him out of it, playfully slapping his back and rubbing his head, and they didn't even hear the winners of the two following classes. But they quieted quickly enough when Bell reached the senior list.

"And last but not least, the champion and runner-up of the senior contestants from section 8 are William Hilton and Brody Reardon."

CHAPTER 12

Just for the Team

SKY BOLLINGER was ready for the spotlight at two o'clock. As the national champion it was only proper that Bill Bell introduce him. By his side, strutting and posing for the photographers, was the old pro himself: the beaming and smirking Mr. William "Slats" Bollinger.

Naturally, both were most happy to be interviewed on WSUN 1100 by radio sports announcer Gerald Gray. And they were *most* willing to talk to the local TV reporter, looking directly into the red eye of the camera. As a matter of fact, they loved it!

These two celebrities had hardly given Bobby a thought. "The less said about it the better," Sky had observed while they were driving to the gym. "Doubt if they even let him shoot."

Trudy Bollinger hadn't said anything, but as soon as the heroes of the family sauntered out to the center of the court, she tried to find her younger son.

The crowd was growing larger by the moment, and she finally gave up and found a seat high in the bleachers, glancing at her watch from time to time so she'd be sure to meet the two heroes at the car promptly at three o'clock.

After welcomes by University's mayor, the chairman of the AAU, and the official representative of the college, Bill Bell took over. The veteran sportswriter reviewed the progress of the tournament since its inception and then explained the rules and requirements.

"And now, ladies and gentlemen, I am proud to introduce to you the sixty-four contestants who have qualified in their respective divisions and sections of the state." Bell turned and waved to the section where the contenders were sitting. A burst of applause greeted them as they rose to their feet.

"Now," Bell continued, "the contestants in the boys twelve and under class. There are sixteen of these future all-Americans, ladies and gentlemen, and they will be called up alphabetically and in groups of four to compete for the honor of representing this state in the nationals.

"Robert Bollinger of University, James Turner of Davidson, Harry Stillwell of Johnstown, Leroy Davis of—"

Mr. Bollinger's mouth unhinged. His breath came in desperate gasps. The kid must have won that morning!

Sky was shocked! The little brat had done it!

Mrs. Bollinger's eyes filled with tears. She couldn't have spoken then if it had meant a fortune in diamonds. She bowed her head in a little prayer. "My brave little boy," she was saying over and over to herself. "My brave little boy."

The Bollingers weren't the only ones surprised. This story had slipped by the local media too. Imagine! Another Bollinger! Then they got busy, stopping Bobby at the entrance to the roped area, and the flashes began exploding all around him just as they had for his illustrious brother a few minutes before.

That hurt Sky where it hurt most, and it shocked the old pro into an amazed silence. Probably at no other time in his life had the voluble Slats been rendered speechless.

All the attention did something to Bobby too. It completely rattled him and made him self-conscious for the first time. He was stressed, and his confidence was shattered. Chip caught the effect from the bleachers and tried to shout encouragement. But his voice was lost in the crowd. Bobby squared his shoulders and took the deep, calming breaths Chip had taught him, but his hands were shaking, and he could scarcely hold the ball when he entered the roped area and took his warm-ups. He missed on his first specialty, the layup. Chip, Soapy, Bitsy, and Speed, sitting shoulder to shoulder, groaned almost in unison.

"If I could only get out there for just a second," Chip muttered.

"Go ahead," Soapy urged. "What do you care?"

"Careful," Bitsy warned. "They might disqualify you both."

But Chip was gone. Down through the bleachers and right out through the sportswriters and the photographers and the officials and the usual knot of distinguished guests to the only spot on the floor where he could be sure to catch Bobby's eye: behind the basket.

Bobby saw him at once and shook his head mournfully. But Chip clenched his fist and shook it furiously, completely oblivious to the judges' stares and the warning of an angry official who waved him away from the basket. Bobby had regained his composure, but in that brief little interval, Chip made more of an impact on the Bollinger family than he could possibly know. And despite the fact that all four baskets were being used, Chip's action had not escaped the crowd or the Bollingers either. Only then did Chip realize that his smile and encouraging gestures had attracted everybody's attention. He flushed scarlet and got out of there as fast as his long legs would carry him.

"Who's that?" Mr. Bollinger demanded. "What's that kid doing out there?"

"I think it's Hilton," Sky observed angrily.

Mrs. Bollinger's heart took hope because she knew how her young son must feel out there in front of all these crazy basketball fans, and her eyes followed Chip until he was lost in the crowd of spectators.

Bobby displayed pure concentration from that point on. He was as cool and determined as he had been earlier that day, shooting with the relaxed, confident style he'd imitated and dreamed of so desperately—the style of Chip Hilton.

"Shoots exactly like you," Soapy said proudly.

"The kid's hot!" Bitsy barked.

Bobby was shooting automatically and accurately, and the fans seemed to realize there was something different about this boy's performance. They began to applaud his efforts and give him encouragement with shouts and cheers. And Bobby ate it up! His confidence grew with each shot, and when he finished, the crowd gave him a tremendous hand.

Sky Bollinger was speechless. Where had the brat learned to shoot like that? Bobby had probably been watching him practice more often than he'd imagined. Well, he hadn't disgraced the family anyhow.

Slats Bollinger was on pins and needles at first, afraid someone would recognize Bobby as his son and Sky's brother and worried about the disgrace Sky had been talking about. But as the cheers and applause for the little shooter gained in volume, the old pro's chest began to expand, and he looked from the left to the right and tried to sit up a little higher so that those who might point to him would have a good target. They'd be able to say, "That's Mr. Bollinger right there! That tall, distinguished-looking man with the iron-gray hair, the one sitting beside his other son, the national champion. They used to call him Slats because he was so tall and such a good basketball player. He sure knows how to teach basketball! He ought to be coaching at the university. He'd give them a winner."

When Bobby came out of the roped area, Mr. Bollinger couldn't stand it any longer. He wanted to be out there with his kid where he belonged. Out there again to tell those writers and reporters all about the boy, to give them the full details. If he hurried, maybe he could get in a photo. Wow, wouldn't a picture of him between the kid and Sky look good at the top of the *Herald's* sports page?

Mr. Bollinger turned to Sky and tried to pull him to his feet, but Sky wasn't interested. Sky wasn't going to put his stamp of approval on Bobby just like that; he wasn't going to share any of his personal limelight with the brat.

Mr. Bollinger pleaded with Sky, but it wasn't any use. When he turned around, it was too late. Bobby had disappeared into the crowd. So the old pro sat down, disgruntled and a bit angry with Sky but determined to be out there at the next opportunity.

Back in Valley Falls, a crowd of loyal friends knew that Chip Hilton and Speed Morris were entered in the shooting tournament in University. The Sugar Bowl, as usual, was jammed to the doors with high school kids enthusiastically waiting for the only part of the program that mattered to them, the performances of Chip Hilton and Speed Morris. The radio was turned down as the next song blasted on the jukebox. They weren't interested in the twelve and under group.

Petey Jackson, the crowd favorite now that Soapy Smith was no longer on the local scene to challenge him, was really excited! "They're coming home tonight for the Christmas holidays. Well, I was gonna pick them up in Speed's Mustang, but Chip's got his mom's car, so they'll come back with him. Yep, they'll be here late tonight!"

"Turn that radio back up, Petey," someone commanded. "Maybe Chip and Speed have it won by this time."

"And that, ladies and gentlemen," Gee-Gee Gray was saying, "brings us to the main event, the senior championship. There's a big entry list for this division. The university freshman squad is entered, and there are marksmen here from all over the state.

"Sky Bollinger, the national champion, was introduced earlier this afternoon. For those who have just joined us, Bollinger doesn't have to compete. He automatically qualifies for the finals since he already wears the national championship crown.

"Coach Corrigan has had to withdraw his varsity winners because it's getting late and they have an important league contest tonight with the Panthers. But the freshman hoopsters are still here and will compete.

"I was talking with Bill Bell earlier, and he said this is the largest field in the history of the tournament. That's the reason we're running so far behind. Don't worry, WSUN 1100—with yours truly, Gee-Gee himself—will stay right here until the last shot's taken.

"The results of this afternoon's competition will be announced just before the freshman lineup against Wesleyan tonight at 7:15. Your favorite station will bring you the complete results of the tournament tonight at 7:15. Then we'll take you right to the freshman and varsity games."

Petey Jackson waved a skinny hand at the radio. "Likes to hear himself talk, doesn't he?"

"There are others like that too," someone said cryptically.

"Bill Bell is introducing the next contestants. Let's listen.

"Pete Holden from A & M, William Hilton from State, Robert Morris from the university's freshman team, and Brody Reardon from the university's freshman team."

Petey reached up and turned down the radio and was immediately swamped with a chorus of protests.

"Hey, what gives?"

"Turn it up!"

"What is this?"

"Are you out of your mind?"

"Come on, Petey!"

"I've gotta think about the boss and my livelihood," Petey explained. "You guys haven't bought a thing since you came in!"

"Gimme a chocolate milkshake!"

"Make it two!"

"I'll have a banana split with all the stuff on it!"

"Make it two!"

"Make it three!"

Petey held up his hand. "All right, if you're sure," he said politely, reaching over and turning up the radio.

"And at basket number four, William Hilton, State's freshman football sensation, is now starting. Many of you must have heard me raving about this athlete last fall when he made football history on the gridiron for the freshman team. I didn't know then he was into basketball, but I read in Bill Bell's column a few days ago that he was an all-state selection at Valley Falls and the leading high school scorer of the country.

"Pete Holden, the A & M star and everybody's all-conference selection last year, is shooting at basket number three. Robert 'Speed' Morris, also from Valley Falls, is at basket two, and Reardon is at one.

"It's pretty hard to keep up with all four of these contestants at one time. Basketball games are tough, but this tournament is tougher.

"The big, blond kid, Hilton, handles the ball as though it were a baseball. He's up to the running one-hander now, and I don't believe he's missed yet. Holden is having a little trouble. Morris is going along pretty good as far as I can tell.

"I like that Reardon kid. He's only about five-four or five-five, but he can sure shoot! You heard me talking about him last Wednesday night—Morris too—as far as that's concerned. Those two kids sure give the freshman a real one-two punch in the backcourt.

"Folks, I may be wrong, but it looks to me as though William 'Chip' Hilton has hit every shot on the list so far—or he might've missed one or two. He's on to the jump shots now. I've never seen anything like his amazing touch. Listen to that crowd—they've been watching him. Of course, about everyone in this place has his eye on the freshman, it seems to me. Now he's at the free throw line. He's shooting the one-hand set and hasn't missed yet—six, seven, eight, nine, ten. A perfect score!

"Now it's the two-hand set. This kid is hot. The best I've ever seen in Bill Bell's tournament since it started. Ten in a row, and now it's the underhand free throw attempts, and he's hit eight, nine, and ten. Another perfect score! He doesn't fool around . . . just gets set and sends them up there and in they go. The crowd's sure on his side, just listen to that encouragement!"

"All right, Chipper," Petey Jackson shouted just as Gee-Gee finished. "Drinks on the house! Who wants water?"

BACKBOARD FEVER

The Bollingers hadn't stayed to watch Chip's performance. Sky and his father just weren't interested. Mrs. Bollinger was waiting in the car, and they started home, each in a different mood. Mr. Bollinger was wondering how Bobby had done it without the help—how the boy could have surprised him like that. He knew basketball talent a mile away. And here, right under his own nose, his own son had surprised him completely.

Sky was sulking, thinking about Bobby and the attention he'd been given by the writers and the photographers and about his father's enthusiasm for the brat. "He's gonna be spoiled beyond belief," he growled.

"What did you say, Sky?" Mrs. Bollinger asked.

"Nothing! I said he was too young for all this stuff."

"Too young? Sky, you started when you were ten!"

"That was different!"

"I don't see it. I don't see a bit of difference." Mrs. Bollinger might have added that the only difference she saw was that Bobby had been left to do it on his own while Sky's every move had been backed by his father.

"You just relax, son," Mr. Bollinger said soothingly. "Remember, you've got a tough game tonight."

"I'm not too sure I'll play," Sky grouched. "It'd serve that old goat Rockwell right if I dropped out of basketball. But I'll stay, just for the team."

What Sky Bollinger really meant by the "team" was the cheers, the number of points he could get, the write-ups and photos in the papers, and the chance it gave him to bask in the limelight of the local backboard fans who thought he was the greatest young player since Hank Luisetti, George Mikan, or Jerry West.

CHAPTER 13

Clear Messages

MARY HILTON'S gray eyes were shining with excitement. She was home! Karen Browning had picked her up the previous morning when she'd been released from the hospital, and she expected Chip home late tonight. As she sat in front of the pine-scented fire in the family room, she thought about Chip. He'd sent her an E-mail or two every day after he'd gone back to State, and she enjoyed her first hour at home reading all the messages waiting for her. She'd laughed out loud when those familiar words flashed as she logged on: "You've got mail." She was definitely relieved about her surgery and, although tired and weak, certainly feeling better than she had in months.

Chip's E-mails were full of news about classes, friends, the dorm team, Grayson's, and getting Bobby ready for the AAU tournament. But Mary Hilton knew her son too well to believe that the dorm basketball team and the shooting tournament were enough to satisfy his love for the game. Chip couldn't fool her with enthusiastic reports of the Jeff

schedule and teaching his dormmates to shoot a basketball. No, Chip loved basketball, competition, the thrill of
games, and the joy of being part of a team—especially a
Rockwell team. No, it wasn't enough. Thankfully, he'd be
home tonight, and she'd have a chance to hear how he
really felt about everything. E-mail messages were nice,
but she needed to hear his voice and see his face.

The phone interrupted her thoughts. It was Biggie
Cohen. Was she feeling up to some visitors, just for a little
while? Would it be all right if Joel, Tug, and Red came over
with him and listened to the freshman game with her?
And would they be intruding? She smiled warmly and
assured Biggie they were more than welcome. Besides, it
just wouldn't be the Hilton home without them.

Gee-Gee Gray came on the air promptly at 7:15, and
Chip's friends were all there in the family room, just as
they had been so many evenings during their high school
days, draped over chairs and on the floor as if they were
at home. And, indeed, they were. Mary Hilton was like
that. She made all of Chip's friends feel that way.

At Grayson's, most everyone ignored the sports program on the large-screen TV to crowd around the counter
listening to WSUN 1100. The Grayson's customers were
waiting for the results of the tournament, and practically
the entire staff was there too. Mitzi had left the cashier's
desk and was leaning on the end of the counter while
Soapy, motionless like a statue, held a dish of vanilla ice
cream in one hand with his other hand raised above his
head holding a spoonful of walnuts. Chip stood at the other
end of the fountain, transfixed, holding his breath, when in
walked George Grayson. Soapy jumped, showering his
head with walnuts before he saw that his boss was smiling.

Breathing fast, just as if he had been hurrying to get
the results, too, George Grayson gestured impatiently

with his hand. "Fireball, turn that thing up a little louder."

At the Bollingers', the old pro sat in his favorite chair, half hidden behind the evening paper, his eyes looking beyond the sports page, listening intently but pretending to be merely curious. Mrs. Bollinger stood in the doorway, a breathless expression on her face. Melanie sat in a chair by the bookcase, watching the family drama, and Bobby stood just at the bottom of the stairs leading to the second floor.

"Good evening, State University sports fans. I'm Gee Gee Gray. Welcome to our pre-game coverage of tonight's freshman and varsity basketball games. Before we get to tonight's action on the hardwood, here's the news we promised you earlier—the exciting details of the shooting tournament that ended very late this afternoon here in Assembly Hall.

"This was, without a doubt, the most successful state championship that has been held, not only from the size of the crowd and number of female and male entrants, but also from the caliber of the contestants.

"And now the list of winners in the boys division: In the twelve and under class, this year's state champion is Harry Stillwell of Johnstown. The runner-up is James Turner of Davidson."

Bobby Bollinger turned without a word and went up the stairs to his room. Mrs. Bollinger's heart sank. Mr. Bollinger grunted, grabbed his coat, and headed for Assembly Hall and the freshman game. Melanie bit her lips and wished she had a family that appreciated her music and dancing.

Chip Hilton lowered his head and thought about Bobby. He must be really down. The tournament had meant so much to him, and he probably needed a friend about now. Chip was disappointed too. Bobby had worked so hard and made so much improvement.

"And, sports fans," Gee-Gee Gray continued, "that brings us to the seniors, and a big surprise to most of you unless you were in Assembly Hall this afternoon and saw William 'Chip' Hilton set a new record in the top division. The new state champion is Chip Hilton, and the runner-up is an athlete who needs no introduction here: Pete Holden, A & M's famous all-conference selection."

The instant Gee-Gee Gray announced Chip's name, the Hilton family room erupted into flying popcorn, high fives, and gentle hugs for Mary Hilton. Hoops had no idea what was going on but enjoyed batting the popcorn as it fell to the floor. Chip's friends didn't quiet down for fifteen minutes, and the good news provided enough material to keep them talking long after Mary Hilton went upstairs to bed, saying, "Just be sure you let Hoops out."

At Grayson's, there was a brief second of silence, and then bedlam broke loose. Soapy dropped the dish of ice cream, and Fireball let out a yell so loud it startled everyone not listening to the radio. Mitzi ran behind the counter and gave Chip a hug, and George Grayson embarrassed Chip by clenching him in a bear hug as soon as Mitzi let him loose. Then all the staff and customers joined in with their congratulations until Chip felt embarrassed and wished he was anywhere except behind that counter.

The celebration might have continued all evening if it hadn't been for the freshman and varsity games. With the students home for the holidays, University's residents had a chance to get seats, and they took advantage of the opportunity. Chip breathed a sigh of relief when the pre-game crowd headed for Assembly Hall.

CLEAR MESSAGES

Mitzi came over to the counter when things quieted down and asked Chip about the tournament entry blank. "Soapy was really worried, Chip. Just what made you change your mind about the tournament?"

Chip told her about his conversation with Bill Bell and what he'd learned from their talk. Then he told her about Bobby Bollinger and how hurt the little player must be. Mitzi suggested that Chip call him, but it wasn't necessary. Bobby called Chip instead and told him how happy he was.

"I knew you'd do it, Chip. You'll win the national too. I'm awful glad for you, Chip. I—I guess I just didn't have it."

"You'll have it the next time," Chip assured him. "If we have to practice twice a day until next year! And I mean it! It was only those first three or four shots that did it, Bobby. That won't happen again. You're a veteran now. Wait till next year. As Soapy would say, you'll kill 'em!

"Guess I won't have a chance to see you until I get back from vacation, but we'll start practicing as soon as I get back. All right? . . . Good! . . . As long as everything's OK with my mom, I'll be back Saturday, the twenty-eighth. Got it? . . . We can meet at the community center at four o'clock. Right? Good-bye and Merry Christmas, Bobby."

William Bollinger Sr. elbowed importantly through the crowd until he reached his favorite seat in the first row of the bleachers directly behind the home bench. The old pro was bursting with news, and he wanted to tell Sky about the tournament. But Sky already knew. So did Speed Morris and Bitsy Reardon. An enthusiastic freshman manager had reported the details directly after Rockwell's pre-game talk. Speed and Bitsy were happy for Chip, although a little disappointed that there was no news about how they'd done. On the way up the runway and out on the court, Speed and Bitsy talked about the shooting tournament.

"I knew Chip would win," Speed said. "He's the best shot I've ever seen."

Speed didn't know that Bollinger was following behind. But the fortunes of their three-lane warm-up drill had placed Sky directly behind Bitsy, and he couldn't miss anything Speed had to say.

"Looks like you don't get out much, Morris," Sky growled. "But that's right, you're from Valley Falls."

"Hmmm," Bitsy cut in, "listen to the world traveler!"

"Who's talking to you, Bollinger?" Speed said angrily. Fortunately, it was Speed's turn to shoot right then, and he cut for the basket. Bitsy was next in line, but while waiting for the ball, he took time to leave another barb dangling from Sky's skin. He waited until the ball was nearly in his hands and then called over his shoulder, "By the way, I hear Hilton set a new record this after- noon. Did you know that? Hah!"

That did it! Bollinger's face contorted with rage. Then his father unintentionally added fuel to the fire. Mr. Bollinger caught Sky's eye and motioned him over. Sky reluctantly trotted toward the sideline. "Hurry up! What d'ya want?"

"You hear about the shooting results? Bobby wasn't even mentioned, but that Chip Hilton won the senior division. He set some kind of a record. You better start practicing!"

"What'd I tell you?" Sky demanded. "I told you not to let him go into the tournament. I told you he'd disgrace us!" He turned angrily away, really burning now. All he seemed to hear, he was thinking, was about this Hilton.

CLEAR MESSAGES

That guy was probably responsible for Bobby making a fool of himself.

Rockwell called the players off the floor at that moment and took the team to the locker room for last-minute instructions. This time, however, Rockwell used the break for another purpose. The managers were there, equipped with pencils and paper, and the strategy board was pulled out in front of the row of benches.

"All right, men," Rockwell said briskly. "We need a captain badly for this team. Maybe he can get you working together and develop some kind of team spirit. You're going to elect one right now. Choose your leader carefully. You want a gentleman, a sportsman, a fighter, and a basketball player. Someone who will play regularly and who has enough court savvy and ability to take care of the split-second decisions that come up in every game.

"We have a twelve-man squad, so I suggest we have three nominations. One more thing. Put your choice for the captain in the center of the paper and draw a line under it. Write your own name at the bottom. All right, now, let's have the nominations."

Nick Hunter was the first man on his feet. "I nominate Sky Bollinger!"

"Second the nomination," Rodney Early said quickly.

Rudy Slater got Rockwell's attention next. "Bitsy Reardon," he said briefly.

"Second," Speed called.

Keith Gibbons got awkwardly to his feet. "I nominate Rudy Slater."

"Second," Bitsy Reardon called.

"Well, that's it," Rockwell said, quickly writing the names on the board. "Now, choose your captain carefully."

There was a little shifting and turning about on the part of several players, but most seemed to have their minds made up. Bollinger wore a self-satisfied smirk and pretended not to see the nods in his direction that Nick Hunter and Rodney Early were making as they went to work lobbying some of their teammates.

The managers collected the papers and, under Rockwell's supervision, separated the votes for the three candidates. Then, while one called out the names, the other tallied the votes beside each candidate's name.

Bollinger got another shock! There wasn't any question about the player this squad wanted for its leader. "Reardon! Slater! Reardon! Reardon! Bollinger! Reardon! Reardon! Bollinger! Reardon! Reardon! Reardon! Bollinger!"

It was a stilled locker room when the full impact of the tally on the board struck home. Hunter and Early looked at each other in disbelief while Bollinger sat as though stunned, but the message was clear. Speed Morris made the first move. He leaped to his feet and shook Bitsy's hand. The others bunched around their new captain, but Bollinger, Hunter, and Early never moved.

A quick, enigmatic smile flickered across Rockwell's lips as he observed the sulky attitude of the three freshmen. The same smile had crossed his lips when he'd seen the slip of paper with "Bollinger" scrawled across the center of the paper with a line under it and "Sky Bollinger" written at the bottom of the page.

"All right, all right, hold it down! Congratulations, Bitsy. You'll make a good captain. All right now, let's go out and play a good game for our new leader. Bollinger at center, Hunter and Slater up front, Morris and Captain Reardon at guards. Let's go!"

CHAPTER 14

This One's for You!

WILLIAM BOLLINGER SR. leaned forward eagerly, confident that the announcer's next words would bring frenzied cheers from the fans. He wondered if the spectators had spotted him. Well, the honor belonged to Sky. He didn't want to intrude on a thing the kid had coming to him.

"And in just a second, this year's freshman captain will lead his team from the locker room to the floor. We were tipped off on this fact just a moment ago by Andre Gilbert, the varsity manager. And leading out the State University freshmen is . . . number 33, Bitsy Reardon!"

A tremendous roar broke from the stands! Bitsy had clicked with the fans the first time he'd walked out on the floor. Now he trotted out to the center circle with a wide grin to greet the officials and number 25, Antoine Yates, Wesleyan's captain.

When the officials completed their pre-game instructions and Bitsy came trotting back, the applause was still at its height. It was a tribute to a small player who hustled and played with his heart and his head. But mostly it was a tribute to his spirit, fight, and sportsmanship.

The old pro literally sat on his hands during all the applause. Not that he had given any thought to cheering for Bitsy Reardon. No, Mr. William Bollinger was thinking there was something wrong. Some kind of trick had been played on Sky. He decided Rockwell was behind it, or it was something those two backcourt grandstanders had schemed. He listened intently for a few boos or some sign from the crowd that the fans were displeased with the choice. But all he could hear was pure enthusiasm.

In the sideline huddle, Bitsy Reardon was talking to his teammates, his voice sincere and earnest. "Guys, I want to be a good captain, and I want to lead a real team. Let's forget the past and all work together, starting right now."

Eight of those players and Henry Rockwell joined in with the little player's wish. The other three remained aloof, reserved, and cool to anything Bitsy Reardon might suggest. But they extended their hands and joined in the team clasp before the starting five trotted out for the tip-off.

Bollinger got the tap and cut for the basket. But fast as he was, Bitsy was ahead of him. Hunter came in fast for the ball but passed Bitsy up. He didn't even give him a glance. The crowd howled and pointed to the new captain alone under the basket, but Nick ignored him completely, dribbling until Sky Bollinger was under the basket. Then he bounced the ball to his high school teammate, and Bollinger turned and laid the ball high up on the backboard for the first score of the game.

Bitsy gave Speed a quick look when they dropped back on defense, but he said nothing. Morris's opponent saw an opening and tried to dribble around the speedster for a short jumper, but Speed kept pace, deflected the shot, picked the ball out of the air, turned, and dribbled up the center of the court, leaving the opponents far behind. Speed could have dribbled all the way in for the easy score, but he caught Sky edging along the baseline and threw him a beautiful shoulder-high pass, which the big center slammed home for an easy score. It was a picture-perfect play and drew an enthusiastic response from the fans.

A moment later, Rudy Slater rebounded an unsuccessful Wesleyan shot, his elbow almost resting on the rim as he brought the ball down. He turned to the sideline and pegged the outlet pass to Bitsy far up along the right sideline. The little ball handler dribbled upcourt and could have gone on in, but he stopped at the free throw line and waited for Bollinger to sweep the left corner. Then he duplicated Speed's high pass and hit Sky with a perfect toss that the big center dropped in after leaping a foot above the basket. Again the fans applauded the play, and the Wesleyan captain called time.

When play resumed, it was apparent to every fan in the gym that Wesleyan had changed its tactics. Instead of a cautious transition game, the visitors drove upcourt with tremendous speed and managed to score. The tally was due more to the change of tactics than to a break in State's defense, but it was the tip-off that the visitors had decided to try a running game. The Wesleyan coach had quietly noticed how State's number 55 seldom made the defensive end of the floor. The visitors could now play five on four each time if they pushed the ball up the court.

And it worked! At the half, they were leading 34-26. Rockwell paced the locker room, wondering just what he

could say to this team. Reardon and Morris were showing the right spirit, all right. But praiseworthy as their
unselfish gestures were in feeding the ball to Bollinger,
the sacrifice was all in vain. They were leaning over
backward to instill team spirit, but their every effort was
only bringing defeat.

He scanned the scorebook. Just what he thought.
Bollinger had seven buckets and three free throws, seventeen of the twenty-six points. He turned quickly to the
shot chart and checked the totals.

Eleven for forty-two from inside the three-point line,
and zero for five on three-point attempts. Rockwell
mused half aloud. No team could win with that kind of
shooting. That was 23 percent. Bollinger had taken an
unbelievable thirty-one shots, made seven, and that
wasn't even 23 percent.

That kind of basketball couldn't win. That meant,
too, that the rest of the team had taken only sixteen
shots to Bollinger's total. Hmmm. *Three and three is six
and four is ten and six is sixteen shots for four baskets.
Twenty-five percent even with Hunter hitting none for six!*
Rockwell turned abruptly back to the team and glanced
at his watch.

"All right, give me your attention. I've just been
going over the stats of this first half, and we're killing
ourselves with our terrible shot selection. Team shooting
is about 23 percent, and an opponent has to be pretty bad
for a team to win with that kind of shooting. Free throws
are four for ten. Forty percent! That isn't even a good
middle school average!"

Rockwell turned around, picked up the shot chart,
and walked briskly to the strategy board. Then, while he
transferred the data to the board, he drew the attention
of each player to the shooting mistakes.

"Bollinger, you've taken thirty-one shots. That's almost as many as a whole team gets in one half. And what's more important, you have hit only seven for an average of twenty-two-and-a-half percent. That's losing basketball!

"Reardon has hit one for three; Morris, two for three; Slater, one for four; and Hunter, none for six.

"I don't mind the eight-point bulge they've got. In fact, we're lucky it's only eight. Anyway, I always like to be the underdog at the half just so long as it isn't too much of an underdog. Eight points isn't too bad, but it's going to be disastrous unless you make better shot selections and sharpen your shooting.

"The stat sheet shows Reardon has five steals and four rebounds. Morris has four steals and *seven* rebounds. Slater has four rebounds. That's all of the rebounds. The two smallest men on the court have eleven of our fifteen rebounds! It's pretty obvious what we need to do!

"Slater, Morris, take more shots. Hunter, stop shooting. Rebound and feed the ball. Bollinger, stop shooting from the outside and get inside. Let's see, seventeen shots in this sideline area and not a bucket! *Crazy basketball!*

"Now, the fouls. Reardon and Morris have four each. That's because they've been carrying the brunt of the defense under the Wesleyan basket, guarding the big men under the basket. Bollinger, get down there and play some defense. That goes for you, too, Hunter. Slater, you've been doing a good job on the boards, but you need the help of Bollinger and Hunter.

"Now time's about up. Morris, Reardon, one more personal and you're out of the game. It's against my better judgment, but we're behind, and you're both going to stay in until you come out on personals.

"Now, get this! If you don't stop throwing up shots like Helen Keller, Bollinger, you're going to lose your first game of the season. That's it! Now go out there and play like *a team!*"

At Grayson's, Chip, Fireball, Soapy, and Mitzi were listening to Gee-Gee Gray. They didn't hear all his broadcast, but they heard enough to realize that the freshmen just weren't clicking.

"What's the matter with Speed?" Soapy asked worriedly. "He's not shooting! You suppose he isn't getting the ball?"

"Sounds to me like he and Reardon have it all the time," Fireball observed.

"They're not shooting," Chip said. "They're getting the rebounds and bringing the ball up the court and feeding Bollinger. He must not be hitting."

"Gee-Gee said he had seventeen points," Soapy argued.

"That's right," Chip agreed. "And how many shots?"

"Hold it!" Fireball said. "Listen."

"And that's all for Bitsy Reardon, fans. Rodney Early, number 11, is reporting for the fiery little captain. Now, the State freshmen have Bollinger, Hunter, Slater, Gibbons, and Early.

"Burns shoots the free throw, and it's good. The score is Wesleyan 60, State 47. There's five minutes to play. Slater to Early to Turner, back to Early—he passes to Bollinger, and he scores. That makes it 60-49. Bollinger now has thirty-one points.

"Wesleyan is bringing the ball up slowly, using the shot clock as much as they can. There's a whistle. The foul is on Slater. Yes, it's Rudy, and there's the horn. It's Slater's fifth personal. That's the third starter State has lost on fouls—Morris, Reardon, and now Rudy Slater.

THIS ONE'S FOR YOU

"Ted Kane, number 52, is reporting for Slater. There's only two minutes left, and it looks like the Methodists are going to give the Statesmen their first loss.

"Burns is on the line again. He's been up there all night. State's over the ten fouls in this half, and Wesleyan will get two free throws for each foul. Burns shoots the first attempt, and it's good! And he makes the second one. The score is now 62-49.

"Gibbons grabs the ball and passes in to Hunter, who dribbles up the floor and passes back to Gibbons. He sets, shoots—it's no good. Perkins grabs the rebound, and he's dribbling upcourt. Kane dives for the ball, but there's another whistle as he fouls Perkins. Number 22, Perkins, goes to the line. He shoots the first one, and it's good. There goes the second one too. That makes the score 64-49, and time is running out in this game between Wesleyan and State's freshman teams.

"Kane inbounds to Hunter—it's up the floor to Early. He looks at the clock and the pass is to Bollinger. Sky puts it up and in just as the horn sounds. The Methodists send the State freshmen down to their first defeat of the season. The final score is Wesleyan 64, State 51. Big Sky Bollinger was the leading scorer of this game, fans, scoring thirty-three points to take top honors for the night. And now, State basketball fans, we'll be right back with the varsity coverage. Stay tuned."

In Valley Falls, the Hilton family room was subdued. Biggie Cohen reached up from his position on the floor and turned off the stereo. "Humph," he said, expressing the sentiment shared in the room.

At Grayson's, Fireball reached under the counter and turned off his radio. "Humph," he said, expressing the sentiment of Chip, Soapy, and Mitzi too.

Soapy recovered quickly. "C'mon, Chip," he said. "Let's pick up Speed and head for home!"

"I'm ready. But remember, Speed said he'd meet us here," Chip responded.

Soapy wearily deposited both elbows on the counter and complained. "He'll probably want to watch the varsity game for a little while and—"

"He won't be long," Chip said. "Not the way he feels."

Chip was right. Speed didn't waste much time getting there. He and Bitsy hurried to the locker room as soon as the game ended and hustled out of there right after Rockwell had told them to forget the defeat and report for practice a week from Monday.

"We'll start all over on the road trip," Rockwell said. "Now forget basketball for a week. Enjoy your families and Merry Christmas!"

"Merry Christmas," Bitsy said dejectedly when he and Speed reached the street. "Fat chance! What a lousy start we made with me as captain."

Speed slapped Reardon on the back. "Forget it," he said. "We did the right thing. It might bring those guys around. What's a defeat matter if we end up with a team? Besides, you heard what the Rock said about the trip. He always did say there was nothing like a trip to weld a team together. Relax and enjoy the vacation."

Speed's nonchalance didn't fool his friends when he walked into Grayson's. But they didn't dwell on the game. They fell into the playful banter that always resulted whenever the Valley Falls crew got together and especially now that finals were over; they were on their way home for Christmas!

"What about gas and oil?" Speed asked.

"Filled up and ready to roll," Chip said proudly.

"What about our snacks?" Speed demanded.

THIS ONE'S FOR YOU

Soapy tapped the large carton he placed on the counter. "My tips for a week! Let's go."

He waved cunningly at Fireball and grinned as he headed toward Mitzi, pulling a twig of mistletoe from beneath his jacket. "Merry Christmas, sweetie!" Soapy said in his best cooing voice.

Mitzi stood on her tiptoes as she gave Soapy a light kiss on the cheek and then whispered, "Soapy, give me that mistletoe!"

Chip was caught by surprise when Mitzi came up behind him and called his name. He was even more surprised when her soft lips brushed his. "That was for your mom. This one's for you. Mer-r-r-ry Christmas!"

Only Soapy heard Fireball's loud protest, "What about me? I'm here, too, you know!"

Sky Bollinger was in the holiday spirit for the first time in days. Hadn't he scored thirty-three points and showed up that old goat, Rockwell? And hadn't he made Morris and Reardon look sick? They'd run away after the game like a couple of wimps! Sitting beside his father in the car, Sky gloated silently all the way home. Thirty-three points! Maybe he'd match his number one of these days. Guess he'd showed 'em tonight who the big gun was and who should've been elected captain.

Mr. Bollinger, misinterpreting his son's silence, thought Sky was grieving about the defeat. "Don't you worry about the game, son," he said. "You just keep on getting your points!"

CHAPTER 15

No Questions and No Reservations

TO CHIP, 131 Beech Street had never looked so good! He was surprised and a little concerned that there were so many lights on in the house when he pulled into the driveway. Concern disappeared instantly when Biggie, Red, Joel, Tug, and Taps Browning poured out on the porch. In the frame of the window stood Mary Hilton holding Hoops. Everyone had been waiting for him to arrive. Now he knew why Soapy and Speed kept insisting on going to Chip's house first.

That was the beginning of a great week for Chip. It was wonderful to be home with his mom. He'd been home just over three weeks earlier for Thanksgiving, but so much had changed in that short time. All Christmases had been special, but this particular Christmas held more meaning for Chip than all the others put together. He was grateful for his mom's health, and his care showed. Mary Hilton appreciated her son's devotion during the holiday vacation. But she also knew her son was still troubled about her health because he continued the endless questions about Dr. Marjorie Nader, the surgery, the recovery process, and what she could expect in the future.

Although she kept reassuring Chip and patiently answered all his questions, sometimes the same questions, her words seemed to have little impact. Then he wondered aloud if he should call the dean at State and postpone going back for the second semester. He could stay home and ask Mr. Schroeder for his old high school job back. It was a perfect plan. He could stay with his mom during the day, and then Karen Browning wouldn't mind coming over until he returned from the Sugar Bowl in the evening.

"Chip, if I hadn't had this surgery, would you still want to be in school and at State?"

"Sure, Mom. I like school, and State's a great place! But I should be here with you while you're recovering."

"Is there more going on than you're telling me, Chip?"

"No, Mom. I belong here with you."

"Chip, Dr. Nader said the test results showed she got all the cancer, and now it's up to me to do what she says. And she never *once* mentioned you staying home to baby-sit your mother. Remember, we made a promise to each other that you'd finish school. So you'll have to let me take care of my part of the bargain, and I'll let you take care of yours. Deal?"

"I don't know. Maybe I should talk to Dr. Nader again."

"Now, Chip, you know everything she's told me. I'm not keeping anything from you. I'm not going to die—at least not in the near future. And it's your future I'm concerned about! Now what about basketball and that freshman team your friends keep telling me about? And, speaking of talking to doctors, are *you* doing everything the doctor told you so you can get your medical clearance?"

"That's a good one, Mom. Yes, I'm doing everything I was told."

"Good. I figured you were. Now why don't you stop moping around this house and get out and see your friends before you go back to school. You're starting to worry Hoops about his leftovers. Since you've been home and eaten everything in sight, Hoops has been pretty much on a cat-food-only diet. He misses my leftovers. He'd be skin and bones if Soapy was here too!

"Now, give me a hug and go see Doc Jones and John Schroeder before they descend on us. Then I'd have all three of you to take care of. I love you, sweetie."

"I love you, too, Mom."

Chip decided to jog to the Sugar Bowl. It was great to sit on the other side of the counter and talk about things with Doc Jones and John Schroeder and all his lifelong friends.

The Valley Falls High School-Alumni game on Friday night brought many old friends and acquaintances together, and that meant another long night reliving the happy memories and events of high school days.

In the morning, Chip insisted on leaving the car with his mom, and Soapy's parents were more than pleased to drive the boys back to State to begin their second semester. Mrs. Browning relieved more of Chip's concerns by saying she'd stop over several times a day to take care of all the things his mom couldn't yet do for herself.

Chip hadn't forgotten his four o'clock practice time with Bobby on Saturday afternoon at the University

Community Center. He found Bobby waiting with a big smile and a crowd of friends. For the next two hours, Chip entertained them by shooting while sitting on a chair, shooting fouls while seated on the floor, twirling the ball on the thumb and fingers of one hand and changing over to the other hand without a miss, and finally, dunking the ball.

Chip could dunk a ball with either hand, but his big specialty was dunking two balls at the same time. This feat required split-second timing, with one hand plunging a ball down through the hoop almost at the same time as the other hand followed with another ball. That was the clincher, and the kids loved it.

New Year's morning Chip again wandered over to the community center, planning to get in a little quiet practice. But Bobby had beat him there. "Well," Chip said, "surprise, surprise! I didn't expect to find you here this morning. What's up?"

"I'm trying to get in all the practice I can before school starts," Bobby said earnestly. "Chip, where's your car?"

Chip laughed. "Parked at home in Valley Falls. Why?"

"I dunno. I wish you had it. Sky's playing this afternoon over in Bay Village, and I thought we might drive over and see the game."

"Did the freshmen get a game rescheduled?"

"No, it's not the freshman team. It's some kind of an independent team doing some fund-raising. Other guys will be there too."

"How do you know?"

"I heard some man talking to Sky. He stopped by a few days ago and said Sky wouldn't have to use his real name and that some of the varsity players were going to play too. He said Sky could make some money, and it was for a good cause."

"You're sure about this? And Sky's going to play?"

"Yes. The game's this afternoon, and Sky's going to play. He took his basketball stuff, and the same guy picked him up."

"Here I go again," Chip muttered to himself. "Sticking my nose into something that's none of my business. Varsity players! It doesn't seem possible. Every player gets the same NCAA lecture about what's OK and what's not. Common sense would tell him that it's against the regulations to play with *any* team during the regular season—let alone to play under another name and for money! Is he stupid or what?"

This is more than Sky thinks it is. A fund-raiser? I doubt that! They'll all be in real trouble if they're caught, and they'll be caught, all right. Bollinger could lose his eligibility for his entire college career. Varsity players!

What could Chip do? He couldn't tell the Rock. Maybe he ought to try to get over to Bay Village and check it out. Maybe Bobby had misunderstood. Where was he going to get a car? Maybe he should've brought his mom's car back to State like she wanted. Maybe Eddie Anderson . . .

"You practice some shots, and I'll be right back, Bobby."

Chip hurried to the pay phone in the lobby and called Eddie Anderson. Eddie was home and said he could get the car. He'd meet Chip at the community center in fifteen minutes. Bay Village wasn't too far.

Eddie Anderson was there in ten minutes. Bobby hopped into the back seat, and Chip climbed in beside Eddie, and they were off. Bobby was thinking that he wasn't allowed in cars unless he was with a family member and that he ought to call home and tell his mom. But he hesitated too long, and then it was too late. So he leaned back in the rear seat, snapped on the seat belt, and tried to make sense out of the conversation between Chip and Eddie.

"What's the hurry, Chip?"

"I'm not too sure I know. Bobby said there's a basketball game in Bay Village this afternoon and that some of the varsity and freshmen were going to play."

"Is that important?"

"It could be. That is, if Bobby's right."

"So what's the big deal about playing basketball on vacation?"

Chip lowered his voice. "Playing under assumed names and getting paid."

"No! You think anyone could be that stupid these days?"

"I hope not."

"What if it's true? Then what?"

"Don't really know. If it's true, all I can think to do is talk to them and try to get them to forget it."

"Doesn't seem possible that a college varsity player would be dumb enough to risk his career for one crummy game."

They rode on in silence. Chip was trying to figure out what he would do if it was true. Maybe it was just a pickup game. He didn't even know any of these supposed players. What could he say?

Bay Village was a city of about twelve thousand people, and it didn't take long to find out that all the adult league basketball games were scheduled from one to five o'clock in the high school gym.

"Now what?" Eddie asked.

"We go in!"

Bleachers had been pulled out and were about half filled. On the court a game was in progress between two Industrial League teams. Chip scanned the players on the floor and both benches, then breathed a short sigh of relief. He didn't recognize any college-age players at all. There were no reserved seats, and Chip led the way to a row halfway up the bleachers. He sat there a few minutes and then rose abruptly.

"Eddie, you and Bobby watch the game. Save me a seat."

"Where are you going?"

"To the locker rooms."

"Don't stick your neck out," Anderson warned.

Chip walked down the steps leading from the lobby to a lower level. Before a door on his right, two men were talking. The shorter, heavier man was smoking a cigar and looked as if he'd been scripted for a movie part as the local small-town promoter.

"Can I help you, buddy?" the man asked pleasantly as he looked Chip up and down.

Chip hesitated. "I'm looking for—"

"Let me guess. Murph Jensen?" the man suggested. "That's me."

"No, I—"

"Oh, you must be one of the Reedsburg players." He pointed across the hall. "Their locker room is over there."

Chip opened the door. Inside a man was talking to several players dressed in blue-and-white uniforms.

"Sorry," Chip said. "I'm looking for Sky Bollinger."

"Not here," the man said curtly.

Chip closed the door and walked back across the hall. Jensen looked at him curiously. "Who are you looking for?" he asked.

"I'm looking for Sky Bollinger."

"Oh! He's in here. Go on in."

"Would you mind asking him to come outside, Mr. Jensen?"

"I guess. All right." Jensen went in and closed the door. A few seconds later, Sky Bollinger, dressed in a strange uniform, came out, followed by Jensen. Bollinger looked quizzically at Chip, surprise completely filling his eyes.

"Bollinger," Chip said, "you don't know me, but I know you or rather know about you, and I think you're making a bigger mistake than you know."

"Mistake?" Bollinger parried, recognition dawning in his eyes. "What d'ya mean a mistake?"

"Playing under an assumed name and playing for money."

"Hey, what's going on?" Jensen demanded, pushing his way between Chip and Bollinger. "What business is it of yours what he does?"

Chip smiled wryly. "None, I guess, except that I'm a student at State."

"So?"

"Well, he's pretty important to the basketball team, and if he goes through with this, he's going to get in trouble and put his team in jeopardy."

"You mean you'll rat on him, don't you?" Jensen demanded, chomping down on his cigar. "That's what you really mean, isn't it?"

Chip shook his head. "No, I'm not going to *rat* on him, as you call it. But if he plays this afternoon, I'll go straight to Dad Young, State's A.D., and tell him all about *you*."

Jensen's voice rose to a high, shrill pitch. "About *me*? This is just a simple fund-raiser for a good cause. You crazy, boy?"

"Not as crazy as you are if you let him play. I'm serious, Mr. Jensen. If he plays in this game under his own or an assumed name, either one, he'll be considered a professional athlete for the rest of his basketball life.

He'll be through at State and anywhere else. He may not know that, but you know that as well as I do."

Sky had been trying to figure out what to do. Chip Hilton again! What was he doing here? How'd he know about this game? He had a lot of nerve butting into everyone's business. What a mess! Sky realized he couldn't play in this game, that was for sure. He ought to pop the jerk right in the mouth, but he couldn't afford to get in a jam now—and not here. Sky decided he'd better wait till some other time to get even with Hilton.

"I don't know what you're trying to do, Hilton," he said roughly, "but I'm warning you right now. You keep your nose out of my business or I'm going to—" Bollinger turned on his heel and slammed his fist against the locker room door, leaving Jensen fuming and sizing up Chip with angry eyes.

"What are you lookin' for kid?" he asked. "Money?"

A brief, bitter smile flashed across Chip's lips. "I work for my money, Mr. Jensen. I wouldn't be here except for a friend." He turned abruptly away.

Inside the locker room, Sky Bollinger began pulling off his uniform.

"What goes, Bollinger?" someone asked.

"Aw, some jerk by the name of Hilton showed up and told Jensen he was going to rat on me for playing this afternoon."

"Hilton? What's it to him?"

"Got me! Murph probably wouldn't let him play, and he's taking it out on me!"

"Hey, didn't a guy by the name of Hilton quarterback the State freshmen?"

"Sure, that's the guy. Just won the state shooting championship too. Right, Sky?"

"Yeah, that's him," Bollinger rasped.

"What are you doin', Kirk? Aren't you gonna play either?"

"Nope. I'm getting out of here. And fast! I never felt good about this so-called fund-raiser anyway. How about it, Andy?"

"Me too! I'm not going to get messed up now. Heck, this Hilton guy could upset my whole college career. I wonder if someone sent him to check us out. I don't get it."

"I don't either, but I'm out of *here*."

Murph Jensen entered in time to hear the last remark. "What's that? Getting out of where?"

"Out of here. We're not playing."

"Because of that nosy guy?"

"You got it!"

"But what am I going to do? What am I gonna tell the fans up there in the bleachers?"

"That's your problem."

Jensen stomped back and forth in the locker room. "We can't play with five men! This is gonna hurt. The fans aren't gonna like this. Look, if you guys don't play this afternoon, you'll *never* play here."

A now dressed Andy laughed. "That will be soon enough," he said shortly. "We must have been crazy."

Kirk said grimly, "Come on. Let's get out of here."

Jensen was standing at the top of the stairs when Bollinger and his two companions came up the steps.

"Wise guy," the promoter growled, jerking his head toward the bleachers behind him. "Sitting up there like a detective."

"Where?" Andy asked.

"Fifth row up. The blond with the short hair. Sittin' between that little kid and another buddy."

Bollinger glanced up and then stopped short. "Hey!" he snarled. "That's my brother!"

"With Hilton?"

"Yeah! What's *he* doing here? Now I *am* going to pop that Hilton guy."

"Uh-uh," Jensen said, grabbing Bollinger by the arm. "Hold it, Bollinger. You're not starting any trouble here. You take your fights outside. You've done enough damage to me for one day."

It wasn't much of a game. Reedsburg was too strong for the Bay Village locals. However, the fans got a kick out of the play of two of the visitors who knew exactly how basketball was supposed to be played. They drew the applause of the local fans time after time. One of the stars seemed familiar to Chip, but he couldn't place him. Then one of the fans solved the problem.

"The big guy is Pete Holden," a fan observed. "I've seen him play a lot of times. A & M captain, I think."

The name did it for Chip. Holden had placed second in the shooting tournament. Chip hadn't met the runner-up, but he'd seen his picture in the newspaper.

"The little guy is Bill Edwards. He plays with Holden; they're both seniors. A & M will be sorry to see them graduate."

"Didn't Holden come in second in the shooting tournament at University last week?"

"Sure, that's right! I'd forgotten all about that."

"Wonder what happened to the State players Jensen was braggin' about?"

"They probably wanted too much money."

"Aw, Jensen's just a talker. He never produces half the guys he says he will. But sometimes the games are good to watch, and the tickets are cheap. D'ya know Jensen gives some of the ticket money to community youth programs?"

Chip was glad when the game ended. He wanted to get out of Bay Village and forget Murph Jensen, Sky

Bollinger, Pete Holden, Bill Edwards, and the whole bunch of them. If it hadn't been for Bobby, he'd have kept out of the whole mess. He ran into enough trouble just minding his own business.

Chip ran into more trouble just outside the gym. Sky Bollinger grabbed Bobby by the arm and jerked him roughly away from Chip's side. Then, to Chip's astonishment, he slapped his little brother brutally across the back of the head. Sky meant to do it again, but Chip caught his arm and pushed him away. "Come on, Bollinger," he said angrily. "Cut it out!"

Sky turned and swung at Chip with all his might. But it was a wild, slow roundhouse swing that missed by a mile. Chip merely shifted his head, gave Sky's elbow a little push, and turned him around. Bollinger was furious when he turned back around, but Andy and Kirk calmed him down without too much trouble.

"C'mon, Bobby," Sky raged. "You're going home with me!"

"No, I'm not!" Bobby retorted. "I came with Chip, and I'm going home with him."

For a moment it looked as though Sky might slap Bobby again, but he changed his mind when Chip stepped in front of Bobby and deliberately turned his back.

"Come on, Eddie and Bobby," Chip said calmly. "Let's go."

Bobby hadn't said a word about his brother all during the game. And he said nothing going home. Chip and Eddie had tried to keep the truth about his older brother away from Bobby, but that wasn't necessary. Bobby knew the score, and he was way ahead of both of them. He'd known the mess Sky would be in as soon as he'd overheard Murph Jensen's deal to his brother. He'd turned for help to the only friend he had who would understand.

BACKBOARD FEVER

All the way home Bobby was thinking how lucky he was to have a friend like Chip Hilton. And how lucky his brother was that Chip had the guts to try to save Sky from making a mistake, which could have stained his reputation and jeopardized his future.

There was a grim glint in Bobby's eyes, too, when Eddie let him out at the Bollinger home. Sky wouldn't dare say anything to his father about this. Bobby wouldn't have cared anyway. Nothing Sky could have said right then would have mattered much to Bobby. He was gloriously happy because the best friend he had ever known had gone to bat for him with no questions asked and with no reservations.

CHAPTER 16

Defeat in the Bleachers

GEE-GEE GRAY and WSUN 1100 brought the results of the day's sports to the radio audience every evening at 7:15. But tonight, as far as the freshman basketball fans were concerned, it was all bad. State's freshmen had lost another one, their fourth in a row and every game of the holiday road trip.

"This is a peculiar team, this group of players Henry Rockwell is schooling in basketball. There seems to be a wealth of material, but they can't win. Sky Bollinger comes up regularly with his thirty points, but the other team always seems to have a couple more at the end of the game.

"This is a most disappointing holiday trip for State. Much had been expected of this freshman team, and although Coach Henry Rockwell has worked long and faithfully, it just doesn't seem to click.

"Fans, the coming week is a big one for University. Classes resume Monday, January 6. The State dorm league games begin Wednesday afternoon and that night

Southwestern's freshmen and varsity visit Assembly Hall to play the coaching forces of Henry Rockwell and Jim Corrigan. Friday night, the outstanding team in the country, A & M, will be here to meet Coach Corrigan's Statesmen.

"Saturday brings the national shooting finals to University to determine the best marksmen in the country in each of the divisions. Many are anxious to compare the marksmanship of the current national champion, Sky Bollinger, University's own sharpshooter, and a newcomer to the basketball scene here, William 'Chip' Hilton. Hilton set a new record for the senior event when he won the state championship.

"Now, on the national cage scene, undefeated A & M continues to loom as a strong contender for national honors, and Coach Rex Standley rates Pete Holden, all-conference standout, one of the best players in the nation and a sure candidate for all-American honors. Bill Edwards, the high-scoring senior, is equally good; he ranks up there with the best of them.

"Local hockey fans will—"

Soapy observed, "What that team needs is Chip Hilton." He deposited another spoonful of nuts on a dish of ice cream and regarded Mitzi. "I thought you were going to talk to Dr. Terring."

"No, Soapy," Mitzi said calmly. "I said I'd talk to Mr. Grayson about his hours if and when Chip gets his OK from Dr. Terring."

"But the season's gonna be over—"

"No, it's not, Soapy! The big part of the schedule is still ahead, and besides, there's the tournament."

"*What* tournament? The shooting tournament?"

"The freshman tournament. It'll be held here, and all schools in the pilot program have a chance to qualify."

DEFEAT IN THE BLEACHERS

Just then, Chip returned with the paper cups from the storeroom, and the two plotters changed the subject.

"Sure he's practicing!" Soapy said aggressively. "Aren't you, Chipper?"

Chip smiled. "You mean for the shooting contest? Sure!"

"You've just got to win, Chip," Mitzi said earnestly. "It means a lot to—well, everyone."

"I'll sure try," Chip said. "But if I had my way, I'd gladly change places with Bobby Bollinger. You know something? He practices more now than he did before the state championship. He's got wonderful spirit. The real basketball spirit."

Chip's statement was indeed true. And if Sky Bollinger had possessed one-tenth of his little brother's spirit—basketball or otherwise—Coach Henry Rockwell's basketball team headaches would have been over, the State freshman team would have been rolling along toward a great season, and the team would not have been torn by dissension.

At that very moment, Sky Bollinger was sitting in the Corrigan living room waiting for the coach to get home from varsity practice. Mrs. Corrigan had been as courteous as possible. But she had long ago pegged this player as a whiner—a temperamental one—and she was finding it difficult to be cordial until she remembered her husband's words: "He's just a big kid without any grounding or foundation." Fortunately, Jim Corrigan arrived soon after, and Mrs. Corrigan excused herself and left the room.

"Here's trouble," Corrigan was thinking. "Now what?"

Sky Bollinger didn't get up when Corrigan came into the room. Not Sky. He was too self-centered to give much thought to basic social courtesy. Respect for his or any other person's elders was important to Sky only when it was to his advantage. He hardly gave Corrigan time to get his breath, starting right in.

"I guess I'll drop out of freshman basketball, Coach," he said sullenly. "I can't take any more of Rockwell's guff. Here I am, doing all the scoring for the team, and all he does is bawl me out. He's got the whole team upset—"

"Now wait a minute, Sk—" Corrigan began.

But Sky wasn't going to be stopped. "I talked it over with Dad, and we decided I could play at the Y and in a summer league to get a lot of valuable experience and some good coaching. Then next year, I'd be all set to help you and the varsity."

Coach Jim Corrigan was just about fed up with all the Bollingers. But he let Sky continue while he thought his words over. His first impulse was to wash his hands of the whole thing and let Sky Bollinger play with the Y or anyone else, as long as he kept away from his players. Sky Bollinger could infect a whole team with his attitude and poor sportsmanship.

But Corrigan was a teacher as well as a coach, and the greatest charge he got out of coaching was setting a player right in his thinking and attitude about an education, sports, and living and working with other people.

"Sky," he said patiently, "you're wrong in all your thinking about State, Coach Rockwell, the team, basketball, and even yourself. Sports here at State are important only to the extent that they're a part of the regular educational picture. They help to develop character, school spirit, and an appreciation for education. That's the complete purpose behind the freshman pilot program of which you are a part, and you're letting your individual basketball playing overshadow everything. Look, son, you've got to learn to get along with other people and also learn the value of discipline and hard work. If you can't learn some of these things from someone as qualified and dedicated as Coach Rockwell, then I don't know where you can learn them. And you've got to learn some of them this year, or there's no position for you next year on a team here at State."

Once started, Jim Corrigan went all the way in his efforts to set Sky Bollinger straight. By nine o'clock, he had Sky's promise to give it one more try. But Corrigan didn't feel he had connected with this misguided player.

After Bollinger left, Corrigan sat through a cold supper and tried to evade his wife's reproachful eyes. Finally, he couldn't stand it any longer. "Don't look at me like that. You know I had to help him. It really isn't his fault. He's been spoiled and pampered by a father who never grew up, one who never forgot his own *rah-rah* days, and he's got the big kid thinking he's the greatest thing since Michael Jordan."

"He's a whiner and he's lazy," Mrs. Corrigan said succinctly.

Chip Hilton wasn't lazy. Otherwise, he'd never have gotten through the week. As his mom's only son, his top priority was to fulfill his promise to her to focus on getting that college education they'd dreamed of for so long. As president of Jeff, he had certain dorm duties. As coach of the dorm basketball team, he was resolved to get his dorm teammates ready for the league race. As vice president of the freshman class, he had student responsibilities. As a guy working his way through college, he had a job to handle. As a top-flight student, he had a lot of studying to do. As the state basketball shooting champion, he was determined to practice and present himself to the best of his ability. And as Bobby Bollinger's friend, he was eager to help the young player toward his goal as a basketball marksman.

Time flies swiftly for busy people, and it was Wednesday night before Chip realized where the days had gone. But he was happy. His shots were clicking, Jeff had defeated Garfield that afternoon, Bobby's shooting was getting better every day, he was ahead of the study schedule, and even Dr. Terring seemed more positive about his progress. Now, he reflected, if the Rock could only win a couple of games and Speed could start scoring, everything would be perfect.

Fireball tuned in to the freshman game with Southwestern, and everybody at Grayson's listened to Gee-Gee Gray's broadcast. To keep Chip's auspicious week going, the first-year team defeated the visitors, and Speed Morris got eighteen points.

Another "broadcaster" watched the freshman game too. He didn't broadcast over the airwaves, but the statements he made led to important sports headlines. Murph Jensen was in the stands with a friend, and the conversation shifted to Sky Bollinger and the national shooting contest.

"Bollinger isn't scoring," Jensen said. "If he shoots like that Saturday night, he'll get beat."

"He's gonna get beat anyway."

"Who's gonna beat him?"

"The kid who won the state championship a couple of weeks ago."

Jensen grunted angrily. "You mean Hilton?"

"Sure, the guy's good," Jensen's companion insisted. "Remember, he set a new record!"

"He set me in my place too," Jensen said. "I had Bollinger, Barkley, and Thornhill all set for a game on New Year's Day, and this Hilton character came in and busted it all up. Scared them all away. I haven't been able to get one of them to play since. You know how small-town fans are. They go crazy over a name player—especially one from the area."

"I thought you had Holden and Edwards up there a few times?"

"I did! They played in the game I was telling you about. Fans went crazy over them too. They were hot! They've played for me twice since then."

"What do you have to pay players like that?"

"Oh, it depends on the kid. But they all want something."

The man sitting behind Jensen and his companion got wearily to his feet, stood there for a moment looking down at Murph Jensen, and then walked down the steps and out of Assembly Hall.

Coach Rex Standley, A & M's basketball coach, was no longer interested in the freshman game. He'd come to University for a speaking engagement and had decided to drop in and catch part of the game before going home. His early departure wasn't to avoid recognition either. In fact, State's athletic office would've gladly given him guest tickets for the game. No, Rex Standley was leaving because he'd just heard a cheap, small-town nobody break up a great basketball team. His team. Undefeated A & M.

The *Herald's* Friday morning headline startled sports fans throughout the state and especially those at University. Chip stopped at a newspaper rack in the library and read the story.

BACKBOARD FEVER

A & M STARS DECLARED INELIGIBLE
HOLDEN AND EDWARDS
NOT TO PLAY HERE TONIGHT

The A & M athletic office announced this morning that Pete Holden, all-conference selection last year and a leading candidate for all-American honors this season, has been suspended from further basketball competition.

Bill Edwards, a high-scoring teammate, has also been suspended from all basketball competition.

No details were given, but it is understood that Coach Rex Standley initiated the steps himself because of serious infractions of eligibility rules by each player.

Chip dropped the paper as though it burned his fingers. They must have been caught doing what Sky was going to do. Maybe in the very game he'd seen them play in Bay Village.

"Wow," he whispered. "They must feel awful."

Chip had been practicing over an hour at the community center when Bobby came hustling in and took charge. Bobby had been giving the orders lately, drilling Chip and sending him through the list of shots time after time just like a tiny Rockwell. Tomorrow was the big day for Chip, and Bobby poured it on. They never noticed the time and never saw Sky until he called Bobby.

"Brat! Dad's waiting out in the car for you, and he's hot! You're in for it, brat. He'll be even hotter when I tell him you've been hanging around with this character."

Bobby was shocked speechless for a moment. Then he fought back. "He's not a character! He's the best friend I've ever had. He's more! He's—he's more of a brother than you are."

DEFEAT IN THE BLEACHERS

"I don't think you'd want your brother to spy on a couple of players he didn't even know and then get them thrown off the greatest team in the country, would you?" Sky demanded. "Would you, brat?"

"I don't know what you're talking about."

"I'm talking about your best friend here. Hilton, the rat."

Chip couldn't let that stand. "If you're referring to the A & M players, Bollinger," he said evenly, "you're way off base. I had nothing to do with their suspension. I've never given them or the game or anyone concerned with that day another thought."

"That's what you say," Sky sneered. "A lot of us think different. You coming, Bobby, or not?"

"I'm coming, all right. I'm coming to tell Pop all about you and the game at Bay Village and how you'd be in the same stupid mess those A & M dorks are in if it hadn't been for Chip.

"Don't look surprised. I know all about it. I knew about it the day that slimy man came to the house and offered you the bucks. And you want to know something else? I got Chip to go over there and save your butt from getting in trouble. Sure, I'm coming!"

Bobby turned to Chip. "Good luck in the shooting tournament tomorrow, Chip. You'll win it, and I'll be the one you hear cheering the most for you on every shot. See ya." He hurried out of the gym without another look at his brother.

Sky hesitated, glared at Chip, and muttered something under his breath before following Bobby out of the gym.

Chip never learned what happened at the Bollinger home that evening. But he got a pretty good idea a little later. He'd just started at Grayson's when a tall man with iron-gray hair and angry black eyes stormed up to the counter and spoke to him in a loud voice.

"Hilton, my name is William Bollinger. I understand you've been giving my son Bobby basketball lessons at the community center. I want it to stop. I'm particular about the people he associates with. Understand? You keep away from my son! You hear me?"

Without waiting for a reply, the angry man stalked out. The sudden attack had been so dramatic that it would have been comical except for the man's striking anger. Chip was shocked, and the employees and customers were surprised and curious.

Soapy recovered first. "What's with the fruit loop? Is he crazy?"

"That's about right, Soapy," George Grayson said calmly, "basketball crazy." He turned to Chip. "Don't take the man too seriously," he said, smiling grimly. "Bill Bollinger gets a little wild this time of year. He's OK, but he caught basketball fever when he was a kid and never got over it. Most of us are used to his outbursts."

State's varsity basketball team hit the jackpot that night, crafting a major upset. The Statesmen whipped undefeated A & M. In the excitement, few people remembered or cared that the freshmen lost to the A & M yearlings. The sports wires hummed with the story of the headline victory, but the absence of the two stars was the focal point.

Chip was sorry Rockwell had taken another one on the chin, but he was happy the varsity had won the big one. That is, until Andy Thornhill and Kirk Barkley sauntered up to the counter just before closing time. Chip had never spoken a word to either of them. Naturally, he was surprised when Thornhill spoke to him.

"We won the game tonight, Hilton. But don't get any ideas in your head that we appreciate the help you gave us by turning in Holden and Edwards."

CHAPTER 17

"You're Fired!"

BILL BELL grimaced and waited for William Bollinger Sr. to be shown into the office. Bollinger had been a pain in the neck to the busy sports editor ever since his son Sky won the national championship. But Bell received his visitor courteously.

"Hello, Mr. Bollinger," he said. "What are you doing here? I thought you'd be on your way to Assembly Hall."

"This is something more important," Bollinger said gingerly. "I feel it's my duty to lodge a protest against one of the entrants."

"A protest? What for?"

"Professionalism!"

The frown lines above Bell's nose deepened, and he leaned forward in his chair. "If you mean the A & M player, Pete Holden," he said patiently, "he's already been notified that he's ineligible. That story will be in this evening's paper."

"No, it's not him. I mean Chip Hilton."

BACKBOARD FEVER

"Hilton? That's strange. What are the grounds for the charge?"

"Well, coaching is a profession, isn't it?"

Bell tilted his head and smiled. "Yes, I guess so," he said. "What's that got to do with Hilton?"

"You ought to know, Bill. You carried the story yourself when that Hilton coached the high school team against the alumni. I was even in the game myself. Chip Hilton coached the high school team and—"

Bell stopped him. "Now wait a minute! Sitting on the bench and guiding a bunch of kids in an alumni-varsity basketball game doesn't make anybody a professional. Some of the best teachers and athletes we've ever had at State worked for community youth programs and coached the teams. You're a little off the beam, Mr. Bollinger. That charge wouldn't even receive consideration. I happen to know Hilton never received a cent for sitting on the bench that night. The high school kids themselves asked him to take charge of the team. He wasn't employed."

"What's the difference?"

"Plenty! The boy received no compensation in any form and—Oh, Mr. Bollinger, this is ridiculous! You're wasting my time and putting yourself in a bad light, especially since your son's a competitor. Take my advice and forget it."

"You mean you're not going to investigate the charge?"

"Of course not!"

"Well, then I'll take it to the AAU."

"Suit yourself. But I know what's going to happen. They're going to laugh at you."

Bollinger rose stiffly to his feet. "You're protecting this Hilton kid because it will spoil your tournament."

Bell's pleasant manner changed. "I don't think you mean that, Bollinger," he said coldly. "I'm going to forget you said it, and I advise you to forget this absurd charge. Think it over! Good day."

Bollinger was deeply chagrined and burning with anger at Bell's attitude. He set out for the AAU office undecided about what specific action he'd pursue but determined to do something about Chip Hilton.

About that time Bobby Bollinger was at home reading a letter delivered by Federal Express. He read it through with a skeptical expression on his face and then shoved it into his mother's hands. "Read this, Mom. You think it's true or a joke?"

Dear Bobby,

We're pleased to inform you that you have been selected to participate in the AAU Marksmanship Tournament Finals.

Harry Stillwell, Johnstown's winner in the twelve and under division, is unable to compete due to an emergency appendectomy.

As third-place finisher, you qualify as the alternate. Please report to Assembly Hall on Saturday, January 11 at 1:00 P.M.

Sincerely,
Mr. D. C. Coats
AAU National Chairman

"It's a joke," Bobby said. "I know it is!"

"Maybe not, Bobby," Mrs. Bollinger said. "You did shoot well. Let me think. I know! Lets call Mr. Coats at the AAU office."

Coincidentally, Mr. Bollinger arrived in the AAU office at the very moment Mr. Coats was talking to Bobby's mother. The administrator paused in his conversation. "Hello, Mr. Bollinger. This is a coincidence. I've got Mrs. Bollinger right here on the phone. Excuse me a second. Mrs. Bollinger! Sorry to interrupt. Listen, your husband just walked into the office. I'll tell him all about it and call you right back. You just get Bobby all set."

Coats swung around in his brown leather chair. "Now that is what I call a real coincidence," he said. "Have a seat. You look kind of stressed today."

Bollinger sat down, and Coats continued, giving his visitor no chance to speak. "I was just telling Mrs. Bollinger that your son Bobby is eligible to compete for the national championship in the twelve and under division."

"What? Why? What?" Bollinger managed.

"The winner of his division at the state finals had a sudden appendectomy last night. And since your son placed third in the state, he automatically moves up to fill the vacancy. Great timing on your entrance."

It was quite a shock. Bollinger's mouth unhinged the way it did when he was confused, and he seemed on the verge of a collapse. Gone were all thoughts of Chip Hilton. *This is incredible!* he was thinking. *Bobby! A contender for the national championship!*

"You probably ought to be on your way. Get that son of yours over to Assembly Hall so he won't be rushing in at the last minute. His division is the first on the program. Congratulations, Mr. Bollinger. I think you ought to be the proudest man in the country. One thing's sure. You and your two sons have set a real record. There won't be another family with two youngsters competing for the national championship for many years."

"YOU'RE FIRED!"

Bollinger's face lit up like the lights on a Christmas tree, and he sprang to his feet. "Thanks, Mr. Coats. Thanks again! I guess I'd better get moving. Imagine! Bobby! I must be dreaming."

Brody "Bitsy" Reardon felt like pinching himself too. He read the words on the red-white-and-blue stationery again.

> Dear Brody,
>
> We're pleased to inform you that you have been selected to participate in the AAU Marksmanship Tournament Finals.
> Peter Holden, a national qualifier, has withdrawn from the competition in the senior division.
> As third-place finisher, you qualify as the alternate. Please report to Assembly Hall on Saturday, January 11 at 7:00 P.M.
>
> Sincerely,
> Mr. D. C. Coats
> AAU National Chairman

"Who would pull a trick like this?" Bitsy mused. "Sky Bollinger might, but I can't think of anyone else. Maybe it isn't a joke. Maybe it's on the level. How am I going to find out without making a fool of myself if it's wrong? I think I'll wander over to the gym. Chip and Soapy and the guys will be there, and I can check it out."

Driving home, somewhat composed by this time, Mr. Bollinger's agile brain began to clear away the cobwebs cluttering his mind. "Maybe they did it to hush up the Hilton mess," he muttered. "Oh, well, what does it matter? Sky will beat him anyway. Imagine! Two of my kids competing for the nationals. Now I *will* get that picture between Sky and Bobby. I guess I'd better clean up a bit before I go to the finals. Bobby! I can't believe it! How *did* he learn to shoot?"

Bitsy Reardon found Chip and Soapy in the bleachers in the same spot they had occupied before. "Just for luck!" Soapy explained. "Now if Bobby would only show up, we'd be all set. Hey, Bitsy! You're a celeb. Know it? So's Bobby! Didn't ya hear? Everybody in the place is talking about it. They've been looking for you everywhere. Go on over to the table and report. You're shooting for the championship tonight!"

Brody Reardon started to stand up, but he didn't get far. Bobby came rushing up, grinning and bursting with the news. None of his three friends took a bit of his happiness away. They let him enjoy the telling all the way.

"Can you believe it, Chip? Can you *believe* it? I never dreamed anything like this would happen. Pop and Mom are tickled to death. I never saw Pop so pepped up. I almost feel like one of the family," he concluded with a grin.

"Hey," he continued. "I gotta go. I'm in the first round, shooting at basket three. Can you guys cheer for me, Chip?"

Chip cheered, and he had lots of help. Bobby was a popular youngster and had caught on with the crowd. He shot as if he was raised with a ball in his hands. With confidence and skill.

Bobby got a tremendous hand when he completed the list of shots and walked back to Chip and the guys in the bleachers. Then he learned the news about Bitsy. "Great," Bobby enthused. "Just great!"

"YOU'RE FIRED!"

Soapy had to take charge then, supervising the seating, making sure each one of his buddies remembered to sit that evening for the finals in the same seat he'd occupied the last time for the state championships. "We're going to win the works," he said confidently. "The whole works!" Soapy failed to explain how Chip and Bitsy were both going to win.

"I wish we didn't have to work this afternoon, Bobby," Chip said, "but we do. It was the only way we could get off tonight. C'mon, Soapy, we've got to go."

Soapy followed reluctantly. "I sure hate to leave, Bobby," he said. "We'll be listening for the announcements. But you call us as soon as you hear, OK?"

All afternoon Chip and Soapy waited for Bobby's call. It didn't come. And there was nothing on WSUN. "Maybe they won't announce the winners until tonight," Soapy surmised. "At the same time they announce you."

But Soapy was wrong. The judges announced the new national champions in the twelve and under, intermediate, and junior divisions fifteen minutes after the last marksman had taken his shots.

Ten minutes after that, Bobby called Chip, and the entire Grayson's staff crowded around the phone. But Bobby couldn't talk. Chip could hear him struggling to get the words out, but nothing came.

"Bobby," Chip pleaded, "what's the matter? How did you do?"

"I—" Bobby couldn't finish his sentence, and a man took over. It was a familiar voice, somewhat shaky but intelligible. "Hilton? This you? This is Bobby's father. Bobby is so excited he can't talk. He won the championship! I—ah—we thought you'd like to know. Wait a second now, I think Bobby's going to try it again."

"Chip! Chip, I did it! I—I mean you did it! I could never have done it without you. I don't know what to say. I'll meet you here tonight. Pop even said I could. Tell Soapy I'll hold all the lucky seats until he comes. And, Chip, I'll be yelling for you every minute."

"Let me talk to him," Soapy pleaded. "Hi ya, champ! We knew you'd do it! Wait till we get ahold of you!"

As soon as Bobby had been declared the national champion in his division, the writers and photographers had mobbed the little shooter. His father had dragged Sky out to the center of all the excitement and had gotten *that* picture he'd been dreaming about—lots of them—right between his two national champions. Bobby, the newly crowned, and Sky, the titleholder.

Most of the writers and photographers saw the possibilities of the human-interest story. And Slats Bollinger, the old pro, got himself into a lot of pictures.

When Fireball Finley came to work, he pulled out a copy of the *Herald* and pointed to the first page. "Nice write-up for you here, Chipper. You see it? Says you're going to win tonight. There's also a story on the sports page about those A & M guys."

Chip and Soapy skimmed through the first-page story of the shooting tournament and quickly turned to the A & M story on the sports page. They read the tragic disclosure in silence.

"How about that?" Soapy said. "The coach found it out right here in Assembly Hall. You gotta give a coach like that a lot of credit for breaking up a great team. I still don't understand why a player would risk everything for a few measly dollars!"

Chip wasn't listening. He was thinking about Sky

"YOU'RE FIRED!"

Bollinger, Kirk Barkley, and Andy Thornhill and wondering how they would feel when they read the story.

An hour later Chip was sitting in the middle of some thirty state champions waiting for the big test. Sky Bollinger was the number-one contender. Not only because he was the champion, but because alphabetically, his name topped the list. Bollinger was naturally the number-one contender in the hearts of the University fans too. He'd been born in University, had gone to elementary school, middle school, and high school here, and was now attending the local college. He was a hometown product all the way. He'd brought a measure of fame to University because of the national shooting crown he held.

The fans were waiting for their champion, and when Sky walked out in front of basket number one, the ovation was deafening.

Bollinger should have been calm and confident. The support of a great crowd is always inspiring. Besides, Sky had gone through all this before. He'd practiced the list of championship shots for years. But Sky couldn't get Chip Hilton out of his mind. Nor could he forget that the despised Bitsy Reardon had managed to squirm in there too. Hilton had even turned his own brother against him, he was thinking. Imagine a guy's own brother cheering for his most despised rival.

Sky should've been concentrating on his practice shots. But he wasn't. He was thinking about Bitsy Reardon, the little jerk who had sucked up to the whole freshman squad and got the captain's spot. He was even trying to get the guys to freeze him out in the games.

"I can't let those two jerks beat me now," he breathed. "Not here in my own hometown."

BACKBOARD FEVER

Despite the mental handicap Bollinger gave himself, he was still a dead shot. But the fans knew there was something wrong after his first few attempts. They knew he was never going to equal the shooting of Hilton unless the newcomer froze up. They gave Sky plenty of encouragement, but the thinly veiled warning in their shouts told Sky that they recognized the danger.

Then Bollinger began to press. He missed one of his specialties, the jump-turn pivot, and the mistake rattled him. Then he missed again. He stood still a minute or so, bouncing the ball on the floor as he tried to regain his confidence. The pause helped, and he ran out the string with a credible performance, but it was not sufficient to win if the record Chip Hilton had made was anywhere near his usual average. Sky left the court with bowed head.

Chip, feeling loose and confident, had nothing on his mind except the desire to shoot to the best of his ability. When it came time for him to take his warm-up shots at basket number four, he breathed a little prayer that the hoop would be as kind to him this time as it had been the last.

It was! Chip was on! He got a few lucky breaks, but he was shooting with uncanny skill and unerring accuracy. He'd been a marked man from the moment he was introduced, and as he made basket after basket with monotonous accuracy, the crowd began to cheer him on, to marvel at the precision of this handsome young athlete. When he finished, he got a tremendous hand. Chip Hilton had caught on. He'd won over the crowd and didn't even know it. There was no question in the minds of the spectators that here was the new national champion.

Bitsy Reardon won the same measure of acclaim. Bitsy was on his way to becoming a tradition at State.

"YOU'RE FIRED!"

The little point guard acknowledged the applause, but he was aware that he was out of his shooting league. He tried his best, but the fans knew as well as Bitsy that the real battle was between Hilton and Bollinger.

While the judges were compiling the results, the announcer introduced the world's champion free-thrower, Harold "Bunny" Levitt. Then Bunny demonstrated the underhand form and eye for the basket that had enabled him to sink an incredible 499 consecutive free throws. One after the other, quickly and smoothly, the master dropped the ball through the hoop without a miss. The crowd took up the count after an eternity, it seemed, chanting in unison: "137, 138, 139 . . . 168, 169, 170 . . . 216, 217, 218 . . ."

When Bunny reached three hundred, he called it quits. The applause he received was deafening, a real tribute to the greatest free throw marksman of all time.

It was ten o'clock before Bunny Levitt finished his exhibition and clinic for all the contestants. The judges were ready to make the formal announcement proclaiming the national champion.

"Ladies and gentlemen—basketball fans—we are proud to announce a new national champion. Mr. William 'Chip' Hilton."

Chip ducked just in time to evade the assault of his buddies, who were so busy playfully roughing him up that they never heard the announcer ask for Chip Hilton, Sky Bollinger, senior runner-up, and all other national winners to come to the awards table in the center of the court. Then, while Chip and the other champions were receiving their trophies, the photographers surrounded them. Flashes from photographers blinded them as the writers thronged around them and peppered them with questions.

Sky Bollinger couldn't take it. He shouldered his way roughly through the crowd and disappeared. But Bobby loved it. So did Mr. Bollinger. The littlest champion and the old pro were the last to leave.

Chip and Soapy headed back to Grayson's to help clean up for the night. That was the only compensation their substitutes had negotiated in changing their shifts. At the door, Chip got a surprise and Soapy got a shock. Kirk Barkley and Andy Thornhill stopped them. Soapy groaned and said, "No, no more trips to the cornfield for me! Not again! That farmer's still looking for me."

"Got a minute, Hilton?" Thornhill asked.

"Sure, what's up?" Chip asked.

Barkley took over then. He told Chip that he and Thornhill wanted to apologize for the accusations they'd made the night of the A & M game.

"We were a couple of chumps, Hilton. I hope you'll excuse our poor sportsmanship and stupid remarks."

"Forget it," Chip said. "You guys were in the dark as much as I was about how the A & M coach found out."

Chip and Soapy were literally in the dark as soon as they entered. The lights went out, and they were surrounded by the entire Grayson's staff. Soapy and Mitzi had pre-arranged the surprise celebration for Chip, and it lasted until Mr. Grayson entered at midnight with two friends. Immediately, everyone froze because the boss was there. But Grayson didn't say much, right then.

George Grayson was a State alumnus interested in everything concerning the college. Chip guessed he'd stopped in to make sure everything was closed up for the evening.

"Don't let me interrupt anything, folks, I just own the place," Grayson said dryly. "I just want to add my congratulations to the others, Chip. I'm proud that you chose my university for your education. Oh, and by the way, Chip, I guess this is just about as good a time as any to tell you that you've just lost your job."

"Lost my job?"

"You're fired!" owner George Grayson declared.

"You're cleared!" Dr. Mike Terring proclaimed.

"You're playing!" Coach Henry Rockwell announced.

Grayson, Terring, and Rockwell just couldn't stop laughing. This was a strange scene . . . adults laughing, Chip fired, every student standing bewildered. Even Soapy was dumbfounded.

Mitzi finally broke the silence, "Don't you guys get it?"

Their stunned faces still registered no.

Grayson came to their rescue. "Chip, I'll say this slowly so even Soapy, Fireball, and you will understand. I'm putting you in charge of the storeroom. You might be interested to know there are no set hours for this job just as long as the work gets done. That means you will have time to practice and play freshman basketball!"

CHAPTER 18

Apology Not Accepted

COACH HENRY ROCKWELL did a dance step and then leaped in the air and clicked his heels. That sure surprised the Grayson's student workers! The Rock *was* tickled! He had back the greatest basketball player he'd ever coached. Correction! The greatest he'd ever seen.

Monday afternoon found the Rock still whistling as he pulled on his shoes and debated the new lineup he would use. Now he had a team, whether or not Sky Bollinger wanted to play defense. Chip would take care of the boards. "Come on, tournament," he chortled, "the sooner the better."

The freshman players had heard all about Chip Hilton. Most of them had seen him play football, many had witnessed his triumph in the shooting tournament, even more had voted for him following his campaign speech for Joel Ohlsen when he'd been elected vice president of the freshman class.

APOLOGY NOT ACCEPTED

When he walked into the locker room, his teammates greeted him with friendly handshakes. That is, all except Sky Bollinger, Nick Hunter, and Rodney Early. These three made no move to welcome him, and Chip ignored them when he saw they preferred it that way. Every member of the squad noticed his long arms and legs and big hands. Players always sized up the new guy, and this one had a real reputation. They casually observed the broad sloping shoulders—an indication of unusual strength—and they mentally catalogued this athlete as one who had what it took.

Chip was thrilled. It was a great feeling to be back in a locker room again, sitting on a bench between two rows of lockers, pulling on a pair of basketball shoes and listening to the old locker room banter. Chip fumbled with his shoes. Now to get out on that court and feel the old ball again, and this time it was not just to shoot. This was living! What a life!

On the other side of the room, Sky Bollinger was sitting between Nick Hunter and Rodney Early, sullenly pulling on his practice jersey. "Well, our worries are all over," he said. "All we need now is new lettering on our uniforms."

"Lettering?"

"Sure! V.F. You know, Valley Falls! Coach, players, high school *rah-rah* stuff. You know what I mean."

Chip never even looked up. He finished tying his shoes and walked out to the court. His spirits were dampened by their words, but they were not enough to kill the thrill of being on a basketball court again as a player.

Speed Morris had a late class, and he was a little tardy. He hurried into his uniform, paying little attention to Bollinger and his friends. That annoyed Bollinger, and he banged the door of his locker.

"We'll be lucky to get hold of the ball now," Bollinger said pointedly. "Especially with the backcourt twins operating and Mr. Shotsky Hilton galloping around shooting every time he gets his hands on the ball."

Speed eyed his irritable teammate coolly. "Bollinger, quit whining." Deliberately turning his back, Speed pulled on a sweatshirt and left the disgruntled trio alone in the room.

Rockwell was careful to let Chip prove himself on the court. Even his most skeptical teammate could see Chip was the basketball player his reputation acclaimed. Rockwell realized that Chip wasn't in game condition, but he knew that his former star was never completely out of shape. So he took a chance and started Chip on the second team in the scrimmage.

Chip scored six baskets in the first ten minutes and dominated the defensive board, cleverly blocking Bollinger away from the basket and taking the ball on the rebound with perfectly timed jackknife leaps. That did it as far as Chip's new teammates were concerned. Chip proved his performance was no accident by playing even better the following afternoon.

Then, with only two days' practice, Rockwell substituted Chip for Nick Hunter halfway into both the first and second halves of the Burton game. The national shooting champion proved he could hit the hoop under fire almost as accurately as when he was unguarded. Chip averaged a point a minute, scoring twenty in the time he played. But that wasn't what sold the fans. They'd expected him to be a great shot. Wasn't he the best in the country? No, it wasn't his scoring. The selling point as an all-around basketball player was his play off the boards, his accurate passes, hard dribbling, lightning interceptions, and catlike guarding of his opponent.

APOLOGY NOT ACCEPTED

Chip's new teammates knew he belonged on the team, all right. But in whose place? Chip had lined up against Bollinger several times in the scrimmages and outjumped him, outscored him, and dominated the boards. Bollinger was worried sick. He told himself it would be just like Rockwell to put his pet in his place out of spite. Sky wasn't getting any respect.

Then the freshmen met Crampton Community College, one of the strongest teams in the state. Crampton was undefeated and had lost only one game on its home court in five years. The State freshmen made it two. Chip netted thirty points to lead both teams in scoring and give the rejuvenated Statesmen an important and unexpected upset victory.

That performance focused the papers and the fans on Chip Hilton. Bollinger suddenly found himself yesterday's news. Nick Hunter found himself sitting on the bench, the sixth man, replaced on the starting five by this new teammate, who was averaging thirty-four points a game, practically carrying the team on his back.

The freshmen were sailing along now on a winning streak, led by a newcomer who rarely made a mistake, always delivered in the clutch, and had what it took to fire a team with the winning spirit.

Midterms came and went, and as the freshman tournament approached, the hopes of the freshman fans grew with each victory. Sky Bollinger tried to hamper Chip every way he could. But Sky found he couldn't do it alone, and he couldn't get any help from his teammates on the starting five. Bitsy Reardon, Speed Morris, and Rudy Slater liked the kind of basketball Chip Hilton played. Who wouldn't? Chip seemed to have eyes in the back of his head. He hit his teammates with the ball every time they got open. He fought like a tiger off the boards, always came up with the loose balls, got his team the tough points when it needed them, and relished in shutting down the opponents' high scorer.

Bollinger was desperate now and decided to try another angle. If Rockwell was so set on Hilton being the big star, so be it. Sky and his two buddies began to show up late for practice. Occasionally, they skipped practice altogether. But they never forgot to call the basketball secretary when they weren't going to show up. Rockwell had impressed everyone with the importance of notifying the office when it was impossible to attend practice.

Rockwell was fed up with Bollinger, but he was trying desperately to get through the year without a showdown with the immature freshman. The Rock wanted his friend, Jim Corrigan, to have a big man for the next year's varsity. So he bent over backward to keep from tossing Bollinger off the squad.

Then, before it seemed possible, it was the last week in February and there were only three games left—Wesleyan, Cathedral, and A & M—all away and all tough. Each game was vital, and all three were must victories if the freshmen were to receive an invitation to the tournament. It was a tough assignment.

The day before they were to leave for the Wesleyan-Cathedral trip, Rockwell spent most of practice in a strategy session. He reviewed the scouting notes and checked up on the details of a number of game situations and tactics.

"We should win at Wesleyan, even though they took us here by ten points. We're much stronger now and better equipped to meet their press.

"Cathedral is a different story. You all know about Venetti, their big man. He's six-ten and he's strong. However, their entire attack is built around Venetti's pivot play under the basket, and I think Bollinger and Hilton can handle him with the shuttle and by playing him from the front. Perhaps we'd better check that."

Rockwell turned to the board and quickly sketched in the situation, explaining the defensive strategy he called the shuttle.

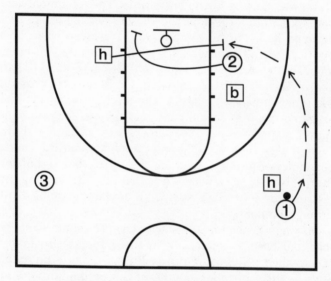

"The ball is at circle 1. Bollinger is playing in front of circle 2. That's Venetti. Hilton is playing behind but floating a little away from his opponent, circle 3. When player 1, with the ball, shoots or passes to Venetti, circle 2, Bollinger, B, will try for the interception, of course. If he can't get the ball, he crosses to the other side of the lane and blocks out circle 3 and gets in position for the rebound. Hilton will leave his position when the shot or pass is attempted and block Venetti away from the basket. Got it? I think you know the maneuver. We practiced it enough, but a little review won't hurt. At any rate, you can be thinking about it between now and the night we have to take care of Mr. Venetti. Now one last thing—these three games are vital. Get a lot of rest tonight. Be here promptly at two o'clock in front of the gym. That's all."

Wesleyan, located in the mountainous region of the state, was famous for its hospitality. The freshmen were housed, two to a room, in the visitors' section of the best dorm on its beautiful campus. And Wesleyan hosts' hospitality didn't stop there. They had scheduled an enormous buffet for them. However, Coach Rockwell had heard all about the special treatment from Jim Corrigan. As the Statesmen entered the dining room for the pregame meal, Rockwell gave instructions for the managers to make sure the players ate sparingly. Full, bloated stomachs meant lethargic players on the court, he reminded them. Great for Wesleyan, but lethal for State. Nearly everyone chuckled at the managers' instructions, but Sky, Nick, and Rodney grumbled all through dinner.

It was a real game. Wesleyan tried the same strategy that had been so successful in the game at University and applied a full-court press. But this was a different State team. Chip took charge of the ballhandling, and with Bitsy Reardon and Speed Morris cutting and dribbling, the Methodist press backfired. It was the Statesmen ran up the big score, made the interceptions, controlled the game, and easily won by a score of 73-62. Chip got twenty-eight points, Bollinger made thirteen, Reardon racked up seventeen, Morris eleven, and Slater four. Hunter, Kane, Early, Connors, and Kramer played during different stages of the game but did not score.

APOLOGY NOT ACCEPTED

Rockwell joined his players in the locker room, proud of their performance. "Nice going, guys. That was playing real basketball. Now, it's early, only 8:15. You can watch the varsity game—they've got seats reserved for you—or grab a bite in the dining room or go back to the dorm if you like. But I think it's important that we set a curfew for eleven o'clock with everyone in bed at 11:15.

"This is a school night, and it's important that we conduct ourselves like gentlemen. We've got a long bus ride and a bitter battle ahead tomorrow night. OK, I'm staying for the game. I'll see everyone at the dorm later tonight."

All of the players were in their rooms when Rockwell checked back at eleven o'clock. Some were already in bed. Rockwell smiled, muttered something about being dead tired, and left. A win always made sleeping easy. He didn't wake up until one of the team managers knocked on his door at 7:30.

The Wesleyan students kidded the State freshmen a bit about the licking they were going to get at Cathedral that night, but they took their own ribbing over the defeat with good grace. Rockwell was in a happy frame of mind, enjoying the good-natured joking among college students. But after breakfast, and after a half-hour visit with Wesleyan's dean, his mood changed. He scarcely opened his mouth all during the long bus trip to Warren, the home of Cathedral.

He shocked everybody in the locker room just before the team started to dress for the all-important game. "Men," he said slowly, almost sadly, "I regret that I have to request four members of the team to sit out tonight's game. I'm sure they understand why, and I hope it will not be necessary to go into details.

"Bollinger, Hunter, Early, and Kepley are the players who will have to watch this game from the bleachers."

The players sat motionless, stunned into shocked silence. Then the nine remaining players began slowly to suit up.

Bollinger stared at Rockwell with hate-filled eyes. "You're making an awful mistake," he said angrily. "But it serves you right. Come on, guys."

Kepley hesitated. "But we didn't—"

"Shut up," Hunter commanded. "You coming or not?"

"I think we ought to explain," Kepley said, shaking his head. "I—this isn't right, Coach—"

Rockwell interrupted him. "I said I didn't wish to go into details." He turned away, and Kepley reluctantly left the room, shaking his head. Outside the door he paused. Then he got an idea and headed for a phone.

The first half of that game was a massacre. Venetti had a field day and got twenty-five points. Rockwell used four men again the giant. Gibbons, Lewis, Kane, and Connors, one after the other, tried to stop him, and all went out on fouls. To make it even worse, Rockwell got an important phone call just before the half. As a matter of fact, he never saw the last few minutes of the debacle.

The score at the half was 49-31.

Bitsy took over in the locker room and urged his teammates, "Come on and fight!" But Chip suggested that they use the full-court press.

"Let's try it," Chip urged. "We haven't got anything to lose. We're eighteen points down, and we'll never catch them with straight-up basketball. I'll play Venetti, OK?"

At that moment, Rockwell entered the room, followed by Kepley, Bollinger, Hunter, and Early. "Hold it, men," he said wearily. "Just as Sky tried to tell me a little while ago, I've made a terrible mistake. Some erroneous information was passed on to me this morning, and I accepted it at face value. I'm truly sorry for my part in the mistake, and I'd like to sincerely apologize to the four players right now."

Rockwell turned. "I hope you will accept my apology and put on your uniforms."

Bollinger laughed shortly, a sneer on his face. "Now?" he asked incredulously. "When the game's lost? Not me! You made the mistake. You live with the loss of the game and the tournament bid. Humph! I like to win games!"

Rockwell's face was deathly white. "I like to win games, too, Sky," he said softly. "I genuinely wish you'd accept my apology and stick with us."

"Not me!" Bollinger said defiantly. "You're gonna lose this one without me!" He turned toward the door. "Nope, like you said, Coach, I'll watch this one from the bleachers. You guys coming with me?" He turned and left the room, followed by Hunter and Early. Kepley dove for his State travel bag and began to put on his uniform.

Bollinger should really have been given credit for the victory that followed. The team came back in the second half with a full-court press, that shut down Venetti and disrupted the transition game of his teammates, throwing them into confusion.

Bollinger's words and attitude had filled Bitsy, Chip, Speed, Rudy, and Keith with hot anger, welding them into a desperately determined team that fought and dove and tumbled and scrambled to a one-point deficit with six seconds to go. As the six seconds started to tick off—with the Statesmen behind in the score 69-68 and with Cathedral in possession of the ball—Chip stole it right out of Venetti's hands, dribbled the length of the court, and drove in and up for the layup.

Chip was hit on the shot and knocked into the third row of bleachers as the ball dropped through the basket.

He calmly sank the free throw for a two-point victory for the team and thirty-nine points to lead all scorers.

Sky, Nick, and Rodney were quiet and subdued going back to University the next morning. Rockwell made it a point to explain the incident to the entire squad. The two-room suite that had been assigned to Bollinger, Hunter, Early, and Kepley at Wesleyan was not acceptable to them because the paint used in routine maintenance had not dried properly and burned their eyes. Consequently, the four players were transferred to other rooms. Some Wesleyan students in the next dorm found the room unlocked and decided to use the suite for a party. They'd been reported to the dean for trashing the room, and he'd not learned until the following afternoon that the damage had not been caused by the visitors.

Rockwell again apologized to the four, and Early and Kepley decided to remain with the squad. But Bollinger and Hunter decided to make the most of Rockwell's plight. They said they'd better think it over for a couple of days.

The following afternoon, Mr. Bollinger was so upset over Sky's difficulty with Rockwell that he drove straight home, forgetting all about stopping at the community center for Bobby. Then he made a mistake. He sent Sky for Bobby in the car.

Bobby had cut the article about the Cathedral game out of the paper and memorized the stats. "Sky," he said enthusiastically, "Chip must have been hot! It says here he got thirty-nine points and pulled the game out of the fire. That last play would've made the Play of the Day!"

Bobby was sorry the second he mentioned Chip. He knew how his brother felt, but it was too late. The words were out, and he couldn't take them back.

Sky had seen the story. He had hoped to find some praise for his resolute stand against the old goat

Rockwell. But there wasn't a word about the unfortunate incident.

"Brat, I told you before not to mention that jerk, didn't I?" he raged.

"He's not a jerk!"

Sky gripped the wheel of the car with his left hand and slapped Bobby with the back of his right. Bobby grabbed Sky's arm in self-defense and held on desperately. Then, suddenly, the car was out of control. It swerved, and Sky hit the brakes and straightened it out too late. The car leaped the curb and smashed headlong into a telephone pole.

Sky, unhurt but panic-stricken, was out of the car almost as soon as it stopped, more concerned with the damage to the car and his father's reaction than anything else. Almost immediately, the car was surrounded by people. Then a woman screamed, and Sky saw Bobby lying halfway out the door. He was as white as a sheet, his eyes closed, and unconscious.

Sky's eyes, frantic with sickening, horrible disbelief, focused on the blood slowly pooling under Bobby's head.

CHAPTER 19

Sky Makes a Decision

BOBBY BOLLINGER was wheeled from the ambulance to the emergency room where quick, gentle fingers expertly explored his head injury.

"Will you come with me please?" The whisper came softly.

Sky didn't move. He stood by the stretcher, hands clinging to the cold metal railing. The nurse touched Sky's arm, pulling at it until she got his attention. "Will you please come with me?" she repeated.

"I—" Sky looked down at the little form with the sheet tucked up under the pale face. He shook his head violently. "Will he be all right?"

"Have his parents been notified? Are you a relative?"

"No—Yes, yes. I'm his brother. I—"

"Follow me, please."

Sky followed as far as the door and then stopped and looked back, his eyes searching the face of the nurse who was checking Bobby's pulse. *My fault,* Sky was thinking, *it's all my fault.* He stood there a long minute, his big hands gripping the hard, unsympathetic wooden frame of the door. Then he slowly lifted his head and said a little prayer.

The woman behind the admitting desk was all business, curt and efficient. She spoke with a cool aloofness that antagonized Sky, and she snapped him out of his stupor. Perhaps the woman's attitude was designed to do just that. Perhaps it was the result of discipline, a steeled resistance to all emotion.

"The patient's name? . . . Address? . . . Telephone? . . . Your brother? . . . What's your name? . . . Address? . . . Same? . . . Excuse me a moment."

Sky glanced at the woman behind the desk and then slipped away. He tiptoed softly to the corner and into the emergency room. Bobby was still lying on the hospital stretcher, pale, his eyes closed, and breathing with labored effort. Sky's eyes again sought and caught those of the nurse by Bobby's side.

"Is he all right? Will he be all right? Please—"

"The doctor thinks so. You'll have to wait out there. I'll keep in touch with you."

Sky sat in the waiting room by the window and looked out through the glass, never seeing a thing.

Bad news travels fast. Chip heard about the accident at six o'clock, and a cab dropped him off at the hospital at 6:15. As he passed the waiting room on the way to the desk, he recognized Sky and Mr. Bollinger and a woman he guessed was Mrs. Bollinger.

"We have no report on the Bollinger boy," the woman behind the desk said crisply. "Mr. and Mrs. Bollinger are waiting right over there. Perhaps you'd like to join them."

Chip thanked the woman and sat down in the waiting room. Mrs. Bollinger glanced at him, warm appreciation in her eyes, and then dropped her head. Sky never moved; he never shifted his eyes from the window. Mr. Bollinger sat looking straight ahead with unseeing eyes. Two hours later, Chip listened as the doctor conferred with the Bollinger family.

"Your son is resting comfortably. He's already admitted, and he's in room 507. He is conscious, but we have to be careful about excitement. His condition is good, but he has a serious concussion. You can see him for a few moments, and that's it for tonight."

Sky Bollinger had never appreciated responsibilities. He always had taken everything for granted. His philosophy of life was the same as that of too many kids. Parents were supposed to provide their kids with good clothes, spending money, a good education, and all the necessities that would permit them to have carefree and happy lives like others in their group—and no questions asked.

He'd never known the joy of carrying his share of the load. He'd never known the pride of accomplishment, the thrill accompanying the performance of a family duty, or the reward of a younger brother's smile when he gave himself wholeheartedly to his little brother's problems, joys, and hopes.

That was a long night and an important night in Sky's life. He gave himself a good going-over through the long, dark hours. He realized, at last, the fool he'd made of himself in neglecting the most precious thing in life—his family.

Later that night, Chip kept calling the hospital to check on Bobby's condition. He was told that Bobby was resting comfortably. And when his condition was favorable, the nurses would be sure to tell him Chip Hilton had called.

The next day the freshmen left for the crucial game with A & M at Salem. On the way, Chip's thoughts were constantly with his young friend. He'd called the hospital just before the bus pulled out, and the information had been good. "Bobby Bollinger was conscious and progressing satisfactorily. No visitors."

Bobby came out of the long sleep feeling as groggy and tired as he often did in the summer months during long, lazy afternoons. He heard the voices and looked up to find someone in a white coat with a whistle hanging around his neck. The guy wasn't the official he'd just been telling where to get off, so Bobby lost interest and went back to sleep.

Bobby wasn't groggy very long. He was trying to get ahold of something important. But it kept eluding him. He eventually caught it. The A & M game! With a display of strength he bet the guy holding him had never seen before, Bobby managed to make it to one elbow. "How did Chip make out?" he asked.

It took Bobby's parents, Sky, and Melanie hours to figure out what he was talking about, and during all that time, the doctor was listening and watching anxiously. "Who's this Chip?" he asked. "This Chip Hilton?"

He found out a lot about Chip Hilton, but he wasn't sure the information was of much value. That night, however, he was reading the sports page, and then he got the answer.

BACKBOARD FEVER

STATE FRESHMEN IN KEY GAME TONIGHT

PLAY A & M FRESHMEN

Visitors' Big Hope Rests With Chip Hilton

Tonight's clash between the once-beaten Aggie freshmen and the up-and-coming State team will be a battle. The University beginners boast a nine-game winning streak after a shaky early-season start. A victory in tonight's contest will automatically place them in the inaugural freshman tournament.

The key man in the visitors' attack is William "Chip" Hilton, the automatic scoring machine who's averaging over 35 points per game.

Hilton is a product of Valley Falls High School and played four years under Henry Rockwell. A & M is out to stop the Blond Bomber.

"Hmmm," Dr. Emerald grunted. "So that's it! I might have known it would be basketball. I guess I'll call the hospital. Maybe a little basketball will snap the kid out of it."

That night an intern appeared in Bobby's room with a portable radio. "Hi ya, kiddo," he said. "I've got something very special here to keep you from thinking about the girls. Maybe you'd like to listen to the basketball game?"

But it didn't click. Bobby drifted away in dreamy sleep. It was too bad. He missed a great game by the Statesmen and Chip Hilton.

Gee-Gee Gray was at Salem to bring the play-by-play for State's freshmen and the varsity invasion of the A & M stronghold to the local fans. Practically everyone in University tuned in to the freshman game that night.

SKY MAKES A DECISION

"And that gives A & M the edge. As we take a commercial break midway in the second half of this knock-down-drag-out contest, it's A & M by the slim margin of one point—57-56.

"Everybody in this backboard-fever-stricken gym must have gotten here at six o'clock tonight. There wasn't a vacant seat in sight when we went on the air at 7:15.

"This is a must game for State's freshmen. It's do or die tonight. They must win to clinch a bid for the last remaining spot of the tournament, or they will watch the games from the bleachers.

"The Aggies have already accepted a bid and will meet Woodmere Friday night. But as you can tell from the score, any contest between these two teams is a championship game.

"Now back to the game. Chip Hilton, State's yearling hoop sensation, has scored forty of State's fifty-six points.

"Time is in. The Aggies have the ball. It's over to Green to Kelsey to Byrnes and Hilton stabs at the ball. There's a scramble—Hilton's got it—he's driving down the court. Kelsey is chasing him, Hilton shoots—Kelsey hits him—the ball is on the rim—it's good! Hilton was fouled, I think. Yes, he's on the line, and the score is now 58-57. State leads.

"Hilton toes the line, bounces the ball—he shoots—it's good. That makes it State 59 to A & M's 57. Hilton now has forty-three points and is approaching the all-time record of forty-seven points set here in 1990 by Curly Regan."

Grayson's customers were having a difficult time getting any service that night. Soapy and Finley were riding with Chip on every shot by way of Fireball's radio.

"Only five more, Chipper," Soapy pleaded. "Come on, you guys can do it! Oh, I'm sorry, excuse me, ma'am. A super split? Of course!"

"And that's it, ladies and gentlemen, the victory puts State's first-year team in the tournament. This is bad news for Curtis Community College as they're eliminated from the invitational. The final score here is State 67 and A & M 66.

"Chip Hilton set a new scoring record here tonight, fans, dropping fifty-one points through the hoop to lead an underdog State team to victory over a team that had trounced the Statesmen earlier in the season 89-61. So, ladies and gentlemen, the inaugural tournament pairings are now complete.

"Thursday night, Willard meets Barter as Cathedral tangles with Mercer. Friday afternoon, A & M meets Woodmere, and State will take on Shelton thanks to the tremendous game Chip Hilton played here tonight.

"Friday night, the winner of the Willard-Barter contest meets the A & M-Woodmere victor, and the survivor of the Cathedral-Mercer contest meets the winner of the State-Shelton game. The semifinals will be played Saturday morning, and the champion will be crowned Saturday night.

"Now, fans, this is Gee-Gee Gray signing off until tomorrow night when we'll be back in University to bring you the sports of the day and more information about the tournament."

Right about then, Dr. Emerald was talking to Mr. Bollinger. "Occasionally, a visit by someone a seriously sick patient has been constantly asking for produces wonderful results. It's a stretch, but . . ."

SKY MAKES A DECISION

That was the reason Chip found the handwritten note in his Jeff mailbox asking if he could find time to visit Bobby. "Find time?" Chip muttered.

Bobby improved steadily after Chip's first visit, and when the freshmen lined up against Cathedral on Friday night, the little patient was sitting up in bed, his score card in hand, following every word Gee-Gee Gray said. He was pretty tired at the end but happy because Chip had once again paced his team to a glorious victory. Lying back on the pillow, he listened to Gray's summary.

"So that brings us to the final round, fans, and tomorrow night at nine o'clock, State will meet Willard for the championship. So far in this tournament, State has been the surprise team. However, most experts feel that Willard packs too many strong players for State to handle. Perhaps I should say two young guns, Merton, the six-foot-ten-inch giant, and his big running mate, Kuester, who's six feet eight inches of sheer backboard terror. When you play Willard, it's always a war on the boards.

"Cathedral and A & M meet in the consolation game at 7:00 P.M. You'd better be here early to see four of the best teams in this part of the country play basketball as it should be played."

Sky Bollinger listened to the broadcasts too. Sky had been doing a lot of thinking and wishing. But he couldn't bring himself to knuckle down to Rockwell. That scar was too deep. He'd spent every possible minute at his brother's side, trying to express in some way his regret. Somehow, the words just wouldn't come. And as he sat there hour after hour, worried and remorseful, he kept asking himself why Bobby would ask for a stranger instead of his own brother. Why, he wondered, was he a hero to everyone except Bobby.

Henry Rockwell had been coaching a long time. He had been a passenger on the popularity roller coaster time and again in his long athletic career, and he knew that what went up must come down and that the popularity of a coach was usually measured in terms of success. So he was not surprised when he suddenly accumulated a host of new friends who were extremely anxious to be of help in meeting the threat of Willard's height.

"Why don't you get Bollinger back? He'll win it for you!"

"It's just a suggestion, but I know the kid would come back if you asked him."

"Why get hammered in the tournament? Why let a little thing like discipline keep a group of kids from winning the championship? Maybe you have to change your ways of coaching to suit this new generation of talented players."

Rockwell kept a closed mouth on the Bollinger situation. But he'd made up his mind that the big player would have to come to him. The Rock figured a team that had come this far should have the chance to try for the big payoff under its own effort. He was standing in the locker room looking at the board on which he had just written the Willard starters and matched up his young team as best he could.

"Chip, you'll have to play Merton. Play him in front and on the side and in back when the shots go up, and you'll have to block him out all the time! He's got you by six inches, but I've seen you play men as big as Merton and cut them down to size.

"Rudy, you're the biggest man we've got. You'll have to take on Kuester. He's a head taller, but you're just as good off the boards. I know his size isn't going to make you back up. All right, guys, I guess the rest is up to you.

You've done it all anyway. Go on out there and finish the job."

Sometimes a disaster brings a family closer together than a million successes. It seemed that way with the Bollingers. They were all at the hospital, sitting there with Bobby, listening to Gee-Gee Gray's broadcast of the championship game.

Mr. Bollinger was thinking that he'd nearly lost the love and trust of his younger son, the one who needed him most. His eyes shifted to Sky, the boy he'd spoiled, the big kid who should've been out on that court, his name on the lips of everyone in the crowd. *Yes,* he told himself, *you botched it up. Now you better pick up the pieces and set this family right.*

Sky was thinking about Bobby and Chip Hilton. He'd lost the affection and admiration of his brother to a stranger. Just because he'd been selfishly absorbed in his own successes.

Mrs. Bollinger was worried sick about Bobby, but she was proud of the way the Bollingers were facing the problem. Side by side, with love and understanding pooled for their common good, they would get through this.

Melanie guessed she was responsible for part of this trouble too. She'd always considered Bobby a nuisance, and she'd never given him much time. She'd make up for that now, she vowed.

Bobby started to say something to Sky, noticed his deep study, and changed his mind. He caught his father's eye. "Chip's too small, Dad. Merton's a head taller! Chip will have to foul him to stop him, and if Chip goes out on fouls—"

"And there's the tap and Willard got the jump and the ball as expected. Kuester has it and passes over to

Phillips. It's back to Kuester and in to Merton. He shoots, and it's good. Hilton and Reardon are bringing the ball upcourt.

"Now over to the right side of the key to Morris. There goes Hilton cutting for the basket—he's loose— Morris hits him. Hilton has the ball—he fakes—he shoots—it's in! Listen to this crowd."

On the bench Rockwell leaned forward, twisting and turning his program. It was asking too much. Willard was just too big.

Chip was having a tough time. Merton and Kuester knew where basketball games were won and proved it by pounding both boards. They rode their opponent out or under, but they rode him. They punished him if he stuck around. Chip's shoulders and arms ached from the blows of their heavy elbows. Well, he was sticking around.

Gee-Gee Gray was as excited as the freshmen, his voice hysterical with emotion. This game had upset the popular broadcaster completely.

"That's three on—on—What's the matter with me? On Hilton. Merton is on the line—shoots—it's up and in. And that makes it sixteen for Willard and twelve for State. State is coming upcourt, Morris to Reardon to Slater to Kepley, and back to Morris. He starts around Nichols—he stops—he takes a jump shot—it's good."

At the hospital Bobby was busy with his score card when Sky tiptoed out of the room. The others were so preoccupied they didn't even see him leave.

Up in the stands, sitting together, Mary Hilton and Mitzi Savrill kept their eyes and hearts focused on Chip.

At Grayson's, the man with the glasses tapped them impatiently on the counter. Then he sneezed loudly. A long, barking cough was also ignored. Then he reached over for the straw container and deliberately upset the glass jar. That did it. Fireball hastily adjusted the volume on the radio, and Soapy quieted down.

"Slater fouled him just as the big man released the ball. The basket counts, and Merton is on the line. He shoots, and it's good. Willard has regained the lead. The score is Willard 47, State 46.

"There's only seconds left on the clock . . . six . . . five . . . four. . . three . . . two . . . one, and there's the horn ending the first half. What a game!"

Rockwell had cleared his bench seconds before the horn sounded ending the half. In the locker room, he verified what was obvious to everyone by the stats on the charts. Yes, his players were losing the game slowly but surely. Willard's height was beginning to tell in the number of personal fouls.

"The fouls are slipping up on us. You've got to be careful with your defense. Don't grab. Use your feet. Block with your body and not with your hands. Chip, you're carrying three personals. Slater, you have four. Morris, three. Reardon, four. Kane, five and out of the game, and Kepley, two. Guys, we're between the proverbial rock and a hard place. I've been there before, and I know you have too. That means we have to suck it up and give 'em everything we've got. Let's go!"

"And now, with twelve minutes left in this game, Willard leads 51-46. Both teams turned cold as soon as the second half started. That could be a plus for State. Time is in and Morris passes it in to Kepley—to Lewis to Hilton—he fakes—there's a short jumper—it's in, and that cuts Willard's lead to three points: 51-48. That's the first basket in the last four minutes for either team.

BACKBOARD FEVER

"Phillips brings it upcourt—to Woods to Nichols. It's in the corner to Kuester and inside to Merton. He pivots and shoots. It's up and in, and there's a whistle on the play. This one's number four for Hilton, and that could be serious for State. Willard has a five-point edge, but more importantly, that's four huge fouls on Hilton.

"Yes, fans, this could very well be the turning point in the game. State has called a twenty-second time-out to talk this situation over. Hilton now has four personals and has scored twenty-nine points. Merton has seventeen points, but he's worked Hilton at both ends of the court.

"Joe, what's going on down there? Hold it a second, fans. Coach Rockwell is talking to number 55."

In Room 507 in the hospital, Bobby Bollinger sat up so suddenly that his score sheet and pencil went flying. "Dad!" he cried. "Dad! That's Sky's number! Do you suppose . . . ?"

CHAPTER 20

Not in the Script

"*IT IS BOLLINGER!* Sky Bollinger! And he's reporting to the scorer's table! Bollinger hasn't played in this tournament. Word around the locker room is he had some kind of difficulty with the coach, with the Rock. Hold it a second now. Bollinger is probably reporting for Hilton. The Chipper has those four personals, you know.

"These two players have been at odds for some time and were keen rivals in the national shooting championship. Hilton was the victor in that encounter. They're both great shots, high scorers. Rumor is they don't even speak. They are bitter enemies. I guess Rockwell will park Hilton on the bench until the last possible moment. No! Hilton is going to stay right in there!

"Hey! They're shaking hands! Right out there in front of everybody. As the teams came off the floor for State's time-out, Bollinger ran straight out to Hilton and grabbed his hand. How about that! Something is happening here, fans! Something that isn't in the script.

BACKBOARD FEVER

"The two kids are still gripping hands right in front of their bench. Bollinger's doing the talking. Hilton is smiling and nodding his head and patting the big guy on the back. And now the whole squad has joined in—even Coach Rockwell is in there—and they're all in a tight circle clasping hands in the traditional team grip.

"There's the horn bringing both teams out on the court after that emotionally charged time-out. State actually took a full time-out not the twenty-second one we thought. Let's set the State lineup for everyone. It's Bollinger 55, Reardon 33, Morris 23, Slater 10, and Hilton 44.

"Remember, Merton was fouled by Hilton on his last bucket, and now we'll have Merton at the line for one shot."

Back in the hospital, Bobby was sitting forward on the bed, score card forgotten, his big brown eyes shining. "Oh, Dad!" Bobby closed his eyes and held them tight, fighting back the tears. Chip had won Sky over.

William Bollinger Sr. couldn't have spoken at that moment to save his life. His chest was filled with a pressure—a pressure that kept squeezing upward through his throat and overflowing into his mouth and numbing his tongue. Then his head was too heavy to hold up any longer, and it dropped forward on his chest. And for the first time in many years, the big man uttered a prayer of thankfulness.

Bollinger remained that way a long, long time, reviewing the past and making his promises for the future. When the penance was ended, the absolution was complete. Then the weight was gone, and he walked over beside the immaculate, white bed and clasped Bobby in his arms.

NOT IN THE SCRIPT

Back at the game, up in the stands, Coach Jim Corrigan was looking down at the State freshman coach and wondering what had happened between Sky Bollinger and Henry Rockwell. And he was thinking, too, what a great job the veteran had done against all kinds of difficulties. He wanted to go right on down the years with the same philosophy in his heart that this man carried in his work with young student athletes.

"What's that, Jim?"

Corrigan was surprised to find his arm was around his wife's shoulder. "Nothing, dear," he said gently. "I was just saying you're great." He smiled down at her, fondly and lovingly. His wife professed not to like basketball. And here she was cheering like a young student, embarrassing him just a little.

Henry Rockwell was in heaven. Didn't he have his dream team on the court? Wasn't the three-man line out there? A perfect quarterback: Bitsy Reardon. Hilton, the best basketball player in the game. And under the basket a big blundering kid who had, somehow, found himself at last.

He could hardly believe his eyes when Bollinger had slid down beside him on the bench . . . in uniform. He had sensed the difference right away in Sky Bollinger. Rockwell hadn't paid much attention to the words. Words didn't mean much. It was what a person had in his heart that counted. But he'd heard the boy say he was sorry and that he hoped he could be the kind of guy Chip Hilton was and would he help him get straightened out? Rock had been thinking that the big kid was already straightened out. He'd patted Sky's shoulder and asked about Bobby.

Rockwell was sure glad he'd continued to have the manager put "55 Bollinger, Sky" in the scorebook for every game. A lot of people were going to wonder about what had happened, wonder whether he had sent for the big kid. So what? Sky was out there, wasn't he?

"I'll say he is," he breathed as Sky leaped a foot above the basket and above Merton to pull the ball out of the air and away from the backboard—out of danger and out on the side to Bitsy Reardon.

Rockwell glanced at the clock and leaped to his feet. "Time, Bitsy!" he shouted. "Time!"

The players came over and surrounded him, Sky on his left side, Chip on his right, with Speed and Bitsy and Rudy pressing in, all bent forward, faces close together, eyes eager and hopeful and leaving it up to him to make the decisions.

"Three points down! Score 59-56. Watch the fouls! Now listen. Sky, play the high post! Chip, drag Kuester away from the basket and do some cutting off Sky. Kuester can't keep up with you. Bitsy, you make the pass! Speed, pair up with Chip in the cutting. Rudy, keep away from the basket. Decoy from the corner and follow in the shots.

"Now, remember, no long threes! No wild shots! Sky's fresh! Get the ball in to Sky and leave it up to him to shoot or get the ball to Chip. Got it? Another thing. We've got to score! And soon! Before they start using up the shot clock on us. We can't afford to let them do that. We've got too many fouls. You've all got four personals except Speed and Sky. Right now, guys, the way you're playing, you're the best team I've ever had—good enough to win *any* tournament! Now go get 'em!"

Reardon took the ball out at midcourt and passed to Speed. Speed dribbled slowly forward, giving Bollinger time to get set near the free-throw line. Then Speed looped a high pass to Sky and split the post on the left side, with Chip cutting around on the right. Just as Rockwell had said, the six-eight forward wasn't fast enough. Chip picked him off, running Kuester into Sky on the high pivot, and cut under the basket all alone. Sky gave Chip a perfect back-bounce pass, and Chip laid it in. That made it 59-58 Willard.

The big team was cautious now and brought the ball upcourt carefully. Woods passed from Nichols to Phillips and then it went back to Woods. They were moving the ball carefully, protecting that one-point margin, trying to get the ball to Merton under the basket for his specialty, the step-away shot.

But they couldn't get the ball in to the husky center. Bollinger was all around Merton, playing on the right, in front, on the left, keeping between the giant and the ball until Merton was forced to move out to a high post. The fans gave Sky a tremendous hand then, to show their appreciation of his clever defensive play.

Bollinger's guarding was superb, but the results were disastrous. Willard was set up for a cutting play, and Rudy Slater couldn't keep up with Phillips. He made a grab for the ball, belatedly tried to hold it back, but committed the foul on Phillips. That was Slater's fifth personal, and he was replaced by Lewis.

"Well, folks, that's all for Rudy Slater and that's the seventh foul on State for this half. Phillips will get a chance to put Willard up by three if he can knock down both shots. There's the first shot—it's good, and here's the bonus."

Phillips missed the second shot, and Willard led, 60-58. Bitsy Reardon took the outlet pass on Sky's crucial rebound of the missed free throw and then, dribbling the length of the court at top speed, drove under the basket. But he was smothered by Kuester, so Bitsy didn't risk the shot and dribbled out to the corner.

BACKBOARD FEVER

Turning quickly, Bitsy shot a fast pass to Sky, and Chip again trapped Kuester, maneuvering him into Sky and cutting around toward the basket. This time, Merton switched and covered Chip, but he couldn't stop the pass, and Sky drove hard for the goal. Then Chip brought down the house by slipping a perfect pass to Bollinger on the other side of the basket. Sky slammed the ball in, tying the score! That lifted the fans out of their seats!

With less than one minute to play, Willard tightened up, handling the ball gingerly. Chip was laying back, figuring he could intercept and make the attempt. He drove recklessly, too recklessly. Chip intercepted the jittery pass momentarily, but he couldn't stop his hurtling body and ran into Nichols. The official called the foul, and the crowd groaned. It was Chip's fifth personal foul. He was out of the game.

Chip started to leave the floor, but he was surrounded by the entire Willard team, who clasped his hand, slapped him on the back, and ruffled up his hair.

At the scorer's table, Gee-Gee Gray shook his head in dismay. Gee-Gee was a first-class sports reporter, one of the best in the business, but he was a Statesman first and couldn't resist a groan.

"*Oh, no!* That's Hilton's fifth personal foul. He's out, and Connors is replacing him. Nichols is standing at the free-throw line. It's another important opportunity for Willard. And . . . the bonus rule is in effect.

"By the way, Hilton scored thirty-one points in this game tonight and proved his reputation as one of the top—if not *the* top—basketball player in this inaugural tournament."

Mary Hilton listened with a full heart to the crowd's ovation for her son. But she didn't forget that the game was the thing. She sat there praying and cheering just as hard for Chip's teammates as she had for her own son, and Mitzi did just the same.

Bobby's heart plummeted. All was lost. Chip was out of the game. "There goes the tournament," he said sadly. "Poor Chip."

Soapy Smith groaned with the crowd, looked at Fireball, and shook his head. Fireball felt so bad he shut off the radio. But he couldn't stand the uncertainty and turned it right back on.

Up in the stands, George Grayson and his wife, flanked by their two oldest sons, joined in the tremendous ovation that the crowd gave Chip when he broke through the last of the Willard players and sat down on the bench.

Rockwell was in a predicament. He needed height. He deliberated as long as possible and finally chose Gibbons. The big man was a hard player. However, he was slow and heavy on his feet. But the die was cast. Gibbons reported for Chip, and both squads took their positions for the all-important free throw.

Nichols, the team's lowest percentage free-throw shooter, bounced the ball twice, looked up nervously at the basket, and bounced the ball again. Nichols let the ball fly. Smack! Clank! The ball hit the backboard, then the inside of the front edge of the rim, and then dropped through the net! An ugly shot, but one point registered on the scoreboard. Feeling more confident, Nichols's shot was short on the second toss and missed everything. Willard led, 61-60, with twenty seconds left to play.

The official handed the ball to State after the violation. Gibbons inbounded to Speed, who fumbled the dribble and went after it. He ran right into Nichols, committing his fourth personal foul. The crowd began to move out of the gym then, glancing at the clock, some in dismay, some gloriously happy.

When Nichols sank that first free throw to make the score 62-60, there were fifteen seconds left to play. Other fans got up then and joined those who were moving toward the exits.

Gibbons grabbed the rebound on Willard's missed second attempt and passed it out to Morris. This time Speed took a good look ahead and glanced at the clock. Fifteen seconds! Two Willard defenders had him trapped in the backcourt!

Both benches were on their feet, yelling at the top of their voices. Speed heard the yelling.

"Shoot!"

"Get it over the line!"

"Don't foul him!"

He gauged the distance and drew his arm back like a center fielder readying for a long throw. Then he saw Bollinger. Sky was standing alone under the basket, his hands high in the air.

Speed let the ball fly; it sailed on by him and went right out of bounds! The pass was too high, far above even Sky's desperate reach. Everyone started for the exits then, many dropping their heads.

The next instant a roar exploded like a crash of thunder. Every fan who had started to leave whirled around barely in time for their unbelieving eyes to see Sky Bollinger leap high in the air and drop the ball through the basket just before Merton crashed into him and knocked him to the floor.

Pandemonium! Chaos! A deep, full, tumultuous roar that grew in intensity until the din was unbearable. Seconds later, when the turmoil began to fade away except for a few yippees and shouts and cheers, the fans saw the official standing in front of the table nodding his head toward the scorer.

The big electric scoreboard buzzed and flashed twice, and the astonished eyes of most of that great throng saw 62 and 62 silhouetted side by side. Against the black background of the big clock, remained a red and foreboding 00:05.0

Five seconds to play! Tie game! Bollinger at the line for one!

Doc Jones, John Schroeder, Petey Jackson, and hundreds of Valley Falls listeners heard that great roar, but it seemed like forever before they could hear Gray's voice and know what it was all about.

Mr. and Mrs. Bollinger, Melanie, and Bobby were sitting on the hospital bed as close to the radio as possible.

Soapy and Fireball didn't know whether there were two customers or two hundred waiting to be served at Grayson's, and they didn't care.

"This is a madhouse, and I hope you can hear what I'm saying. I know I'm talking because my lips are moving, and I'll try to explain what happened.

"Morris threw the ball out of bounds—into the crowd. Phillips got the ball from the official and passed in to Nichols—or I should say—*tried* to pass to Nichols.

"Bollinger had turned his back and had taken a few deceptive steps upcourt, but at just the right second, he pivoted, jumped, and intercepted the ball.

"Not many people in this mad crowd even saw the play, but it was great anticipation and, if you're a State fan, a case of being at the right place at the right time. And Sky Bollinger is certainly at the right place at the right time! He took one long step, and just as he released the ball, he was fouled by Merton. The shot was good, and now he has one free throw coming.

"So, fans, the score is all tied at 62, and there are exactly five seconds left to play. Sky Bollinger, a story-book hero if there ever was one, is standing on the free throw line with one chance to win this game or it could be overtime.

"We'll know in just a matter of seconds now whether this game is going into overtime. Bollinger has the ball—he's bouncing it on the line—he shoots. It's up and—"

Gee-Gee Gray's listeners didn't have to be told what had happened. The steady roar of State's fans confirmed the basket.

"The score now is 63-62, fans, and this game is not over. Believe it or not, there is still time for one more play, and they are trying to clear the floor.

"Yes, there is still time for one more play because time is not in; the clock doesn't start until the ball is thrown in from out of bounds and touched by a player. They're ready now. Merton is directly under the Willard basket. They're going to try a tip-in play. Bollinger is in front of him, there's the pass, Bollinger and Merton leap—Bollinger comes down with the ball and passes to Speed. The horn sounds!

"STATE WINS! Yes, the Cinderella team of the tour-nament wins this thrill-packed game and the champi-onship by one of the cleverest plays ever seen on a basket-ball court. The crowd has Hilton and Bollinger up on their shoulders, riding above the wildest, maddest, loudest, cra-ziest mob of fans who ever saw a backboard. Now you understand University, its fans, and backboard fever!"

Chip and Sky got down somehow and fought their way through the jubilant throng to the locker room. A crowd of freshmen had Rockwell up on a table, and noth-ing would satisfy them or anyone else until Chip and Sky were up there too. That's where the photographers and sportswriters found them. Most of Chip's buddies were in that locker room too. Biggie, Red, Joel, Tug, and so many others he couldn't count them.

An hour later, Chip and Sky took a cab to the hospital. They tiptoed down the corridor, but Bobby had heard the elevator doors open, and he knew it was them. Mr. Bollinger opened the door and threw one arm proudly around Sky's shoulder and then extended his other hand to Chip.

Bobby, kneeling on the bed, was looking at Sky with such admiration that it brought tears to Sky's eyes. The big brother tried to talk, but the words just wouldn't come. Bobby understood why and threw his arms around his brother and clasped him tightly to his chest while his mother, standing on the other side of the bed, smiled happily.

Mr. Bollinger was standing there, too, looking at his two sons with a feeling of pride he'd never experienced before. And he wasn't thinking about basketball at all. Sky was too tired to think, but he was happier than he'd ever been in his life.

As Bobby squeezed Sky with all his might, his proud, brown eyes were thanking Chip from the bottom of his heart, expressing all the things a boy can say without words when he communes with a friend.

• • •

The *Fence Busters* is what they called the famous freshman baseball team the year Chip Hilton was on it. And that's the title of the next Chip Hilton story. Don't miss it!

Afterword

WHEN INTRODUCED at a New York banquet after receiving honors from the White House, Congress, the State and City of New York, and his peers, he said, "Clair Bee, Clair Bee. I'm tired of hearing of Clair Bee! I never considered myself a good coach. I always considered myself a good teacher."

That he was, a teacher. Coach Clair Bee used sports to transform boys into men. He taught them to live a life of meaning—one dedicated to higher principles where values and truth were the foundation on which we evolve.

What did Clair Bee think of education? He had to borrow shoes and a jacket to graduate from high school in West Virginia. He lost his parents and from the age of twelve was the main means of support for his grandmother and younger sisters and brothers. He made sure his players—his "boys"—had an easier time with education.

Clair Bee took these values to be learned in life and used fiction to inspire boys and young men. He named his hero Chip Hilton. Chip didn't always win every game, but he was able to confront the experiences of life and learn from them in a positive manner.

Being a hotshot junior college all-American, I had the opportunity of choosing what university I wanted to attend. Clair Bee offered perhaps the least attractive scholarship, but I made the best decision of my life to accept that and attend Long Island University to be tutored by Clair Francis Bee. Of course, the fact that the LIU team was always rated in the Top 10 and played most of their games at Madison Square Garden certainly had an effect on a kid from southern California. But I received no money, no car, no perks, just a college education. I learned more about basketball the first week under the Coach than I had ever known in my entire life. But the best part was taking a giant step forward on my path in life.

Every basketball player who attended LIU had a four-year scholarship. When I arrived at school, a huge seven-foot-two-inch player was graduating. He had finished four years at the university and had never played one minute in a game. Clair Bee gave up on him ever playing on the team, but he didn't give up on him. This young man later became an outstanding attorney.

At LIU, all of us lived in the dorm. The Bee family also lived there. Every night the coach would come by to see if we were studying. Mrs. Bee, a former nurse, took care of all the players if we needed anything; she was our surrogate Mom.

No wonder every player's parents loved the Bee family. And every player graduated. This was nonnegotiable. One time, a professor called Bee and said that his best player, a first string all-American had done very poorly on the final exam. The professor asked Bee what he should do. Bee's answer: "Flunk him." This meant that Bee's best player would sit on the bench for the rest of the season. To Bee, education was more important than playing a game.

Now, the Chip Hilton books are ready for another generation. Perhaps they are needed by young people in our society more than ever before.

I know the Coach is looking down from his lofty porch in heaven and can't wait for the readers to be entertained. But you will also receive what all of us at LIU learned when we read the sign that hung over the door as we left the locker room and went onto the practice floor. It read, Winning is 99% perspiration. 1% inspiration.

I loved Clair Bee. I hope you enjoy his stories.

HAL UPLINGER
Uplinger Enterprises,
Long Island University Class of 1951

Your Score Card

I have   I expect to
read: to read:

____   ____   1. ***Touchdown Pass:*** The first story in the series, which introduces you to William "Chip" Hilton and all his friends at Valley Falls High during an exciting football season.

____   ____   2. ***Championship Ball:*** With a broken ankle and an unquenchable spirit, Chip wins the state basketball championship and an even greater victory over himself.

____   ____   3. ***Strike Three!*** In the hour of his team's greatest need, Chip Hilton takes to the mound and puts the Big Reds in line for all-state honors.

____   ____   4. ***Clutch Hitter!*** Chip's summer job at the Mansfield Steel Company gives him a chance to play baseball on the famous Steeler team where he uses his head as well as his war club.

BACKBOARD FEVER

I have I expect to
read: to read:

____   ____   5. ***A Pass and a Prayer:*** Chip's last football season is a real challenge as conditions for the Big Reds deteriorate and somehow he must keep the team together for their coach.

____   ____   6. ***Hoop Crazy:*** When three-point fever spreads to the Valley Falls basketball varsity, Chip Hilton has to do something, and do it fast!

____   ____   7. ***Pitchers' Duel:*** Valley Falls participates in the state baseball tournament, and Chip Hilton pitches in a nineteen-inning struggle fans will long remember. The Big Reds year-end banquet isn't to be missed!

____   ____   8. ***Dugout Jinx:*** Chip's graduated and has one more high school game before beginning a summer internship with a minor league team during its battle for the league pennant.

____   ____   9. ***Freshman Quarterback:*** Early autumn finds Chip Hilton and four of his Valley Falls friends at Camp Sundown, the temporary site of State University's freshman and varsity football teams. Join them in Jefferson Hall to share the successes, disappointments, and pranks as they begin their freshman year.

____   ____   10. ***Backboard Fever:*** It's nonstop basketball excitement! Chip and Mary Hilton face a personal crisis. The Bollingers discover what it means to be a family but not until tragedy strikes their two sons.

Visit your local bookstore or contact
Broadman & Holman Publishers for all these books!